The Brand-Burners

Veteran gunfighter, Tom Dix, and retired US marshal Dan Shaw finally found a place to settle in Wyoming. After a year, their small ranch could boast twenty white-faced steers. Then one morning, as Dix rides out to check the herd on the range, he discovers that they have been rustled.

Dix sets off alone on the trail of the rustlers and finds it leads to the sprawling cattle-town of Cheyenne. As the long night turns into a new day, Dix finds that there is even more to the well-organized gang than he first imagined. When he is joined by Dan and old friend Wild Bill Hickok, they find themselves battling for their very lives.

It is a matter of life and death when your foes are the deadly Brand-Burners.

By the same author

Death on the Dixie
Ghost of the Gunfighter
West of the Pecos

The Brand-Burners

WALT KEENE

ROBERT HALE · LONDON

First published in Great Britain 2004

ISBN 0 7090 7587 1

Robert Hale Limited
Clerkenwell House
Clerkenwell Green
London EC1R 0HT

Typeset by
Derek Doyle & Associates, Liverpool.
Printed and bound in Great Britain by
Antony Rowe Limited, Wiltshire

Dedicated with thanks to Maxine Hansen

R.M.
2

ONE

There was a storm brewing. Tom Dix reined in his quarter horse and rubbed the dust from his weathered features with the back of his gloved left hand. His wrinkled eyes narrowed as he stared into the blinding reflections that danced across the wide shallow waterway.

Where were they?

Dix raised himself up until he was balanced in his leather stirrups, allowing the reins to take his weight. He pulled the brim of his Stetson down trying to shield his eyes from the dancing light.

The brush beyond the North Platte River was dense and colourful but held no answers to the exhausted rider. They had to be out there somewhere, he told himself.

Dix strained to either see or hear something above the noisy birds which swooped all around, chasing the flies, desperate to find a meal before the low sun finally set.

But it was impossible. Whoever he was chasing had disappeared into the trees and wild brush long ago. Yet every fibre of his being told him that he was closer to them now than he had been only a few hours earlier.

He lowered himself until he was seated again. He gathered up his reins and looped them around the saddle horn. Dix knew that it would soon be sundown as his eyes scanned the panoramic scene before him. Every ounce of his common sense told him that he ought to turn the horse around and return to his ranch, but there was a fire in his belly.

It refused to allow him to turn back.

He was being lured ever onward.

Dix's keen eyes could tell that his entire herd of just twenty steers had been ushered across the river by at least eight riders. The hoof-tracks of the rustlers' mounts were sunk deep into the mud all around him. They had flanked his white-faced cattle all the way from his ranch to the river. There was no way of telling how many other horsemen had been behind the steers.

Too many rustlers for one man to follow, he told himself. Yet he was no ordinary man. The handsome guns in the luxurious holsters were proof of that.

He had twelve bullets in the chambers of his Colts. If there were a dozen rustlers, Dix knew that his expert handling of the weapons would ensure he ought to be able to hit each of them.

Black clouds fringed the vast sky above him as if trying to steal the sunset's glory. Distant rumblings in the heavens made the experienced rider wary of what lay ahead of him. He reached for his canteen and lifted it. He unscrewed its stopper and raised it to his dry lips.

Dix was thoughtful as he drank the cool liquid. Again he studied the land across the river. He knew that he would probably face more than one storm before the start of the new day: one brewed by nature, the other sparked between himself and whoever it was who had stolen his cattle.

Ten miles straight ahead, beyond the wall of brush, he knew that there was the town of Cheyenne. A bustling metropolis of more than 20,000 souls who all relied in some degree or another upon the steers which were brought there to be auctioned to the highest bidder. Then they would be shipped either east or west on the cattle trains belonging to the Union Pacific Railroad.

The horseman stared hard, again looking for any sign of smoke that might give away the location of the cattle-rustlers. He could not see any. Dix knew that most rustlers would alter the brands of their stolen cattle before daring to take them near the agents and buyers. But to change a brand you needed a fire hot enough to heat up your long irons. His dogged pursuit had probably been spotted by the rustlers, he thought. They had not had time to do anything except flee his relentless trailing of them.

Dix leaned over the shoulder of the horse and lowered the canteen into the shallow river. He held on to the long leather strap and allowed the ice-cold water to fill it before he hoisted it again.

He returned its stopper to the neck of the canteen and hung it over the saddle horn. It hung over the coiled rope against the fender next to the rider's right leg.

Tom Dix had ridden a hard trail since leaving the small ranch house he and his friend, retired lawman Dan Shaw had built on the 1,000-acre ranch set amid the wild Wyoming terrain. They had managed to increase their stock of white-faced cattle from the bull and ten cows they had originally purchased to more than twenty. The pair of novice ranchers kept their prized white-faced bull in a makeshift corral near their house and allowed the rest of the herd to roam freely over the 1,000 acres, finding the sweet grass shoots they craved.

For more than a year the two men had worked hard to establish themselves in the thriving cattle business, but they knew that they would not have enough stock to drive east to market for another eighteen months or so.

Dix put his gloves on again. He knew that to continue alone was probably suicidal and it would be the first time since he and Dan Shaw had settled in this tough land that he had travelled on his own since being released from prison.

Yet his still-keen eyes had followed the trail to this spot and he knew that the thieves had driven every one of his precious steers to this point and beyond.

The rider wondered whether the men he sought figured that he would stop trailing them at the river's edge. For if they thought that water would stop him, they were wrong.

There had been a lot of cattle-rustling going on over the past few months, but until now it had not affected his tiny herd of young white-faced steers.

Now it had become personal.

The day had started out normally for the one-time gunfighter as he left Dan Shaw to tend to chores around the small ranch house and corral. It had become a ritual for Dix to head out just before dawn and check that every one of their steers were still on the 1,000-acre spread.

Yet it had become obvious to the rider after more than two hours that none of their stock was anywhere to be found. By the time the hands on his golden hunter pocket-watch had reached ten, he was certain that his stock had been rustled.

By noon he had found a trail carved out through the sweet lush grass, which he had followed like a hound on the scent of fox.

Tom Dix flicked the safety loops off his prized Colts and drew them from the hand-tooled holsters. It had been more than a year since he had last fired them in anger, but he knew that he might soon need to practise his once-expert skills again. The guns gleamed in the dying rays of the setting sun; evidence that Dix still kept them fully oiled and cleaned.

It had become a habit, one that he had learned twenty years earlier when he made his living as a gunfighter who hired his skills out to anyone who would pay the right price. Now keeping the deadly weapons in pristine condition was something he did instinctively without a second thought.

When satisfied that both guns were in perfect working order and loaded for action, Dix slid them back into their well-oiled holsters. Men who made their living as gunfighters knew that lubricated holsters allowed the weapons to be drawn a split second faster than dry ones. A fraction of a second could mean the difference between life and death.

Tom Dix left the safety loops off the gun hammers, knowing that he might have to use his guns again at any time once he crossed the river.

The brilliant sun sank below the horizon as Tom Dix unwrapped his reins and tapped his spurs gently into the flesh of his quarter horse. The well-trained animal stepped into the river and walked across its breadth.

As the red hues gave way to countless stars above him, the rider knew that he had no time to return to his ranch and inform Dan Shaw of what had happened and what he intended to do.

There were men out there somewhere ahead who were skilled in altering the brands of most of the steers who roamed the vast Wyoming grasslands to match their own.

Tom Dix urged his mount on through the fast-flowing shallow water.

He knew that he was heading into dangerous territory and the black clouds which continued to rumble in the distance flashed as lightning forked from their angry hearts.

But Tom Dix feared little.

Soon he might come face to face with the men known as brand-burners.

The brand-burners were a breed of thieves not to be taken lightly, but then, neither was Tom Dix.

TWO

Cheyenne was big. No other town in Wyoming came even close to it in size or sheer numbers of citizens. There were no casual drifters here. Every person within its boundaries had something to do with the business of buying and selling cattle for consumption in the distant cities to the east or west.

Cheyenne's population relied on the money generated from the hundreds of stockyards dotted along the railtracks. There were no larger saloons or busier gaming-houses than those in the sprawling cattle town. The hotels and banks were brick-built as were most of the stores which spread out from the centre of the the town. With the coming of the gleaming railtracks, Cheyenne had quickly turned from just another remote township into a prosperous community.

It now rivalled the original cattle towns of Dodge City, Abilene and Kansas City. Even Texas cattle-drives headed for Cheyenne using the less troublesome Goodnight-Loving Trail instead of the more favoured Chisholm Trail.

Money flowed like water and there were plenty of willing drinkers from the seemingly bottomless well.

Yet for all its wealth it was a brutal, unforgiving town.

Devoid of anything resembling humanity, it was still a place into which men continued to ride willingly, men driven by greed and total disregard for those they despised. If there had ever been decent people in Cheyenne they had probably high-tailed it when the first railtracks were laid.

Countless street-lights illuminated the town as Tom Dix aimed the quarter horse into the outskirts of Cheyenne. His eyes darted all about him at the multitude of people moving in every direction from one place of pleasure to another. Large towns made the solitary horseman nervous.

A bead of sweat trickled down his face as his mind drifted back to a time when he had entered another town many years earlier.

A lifetime ago.

It had been a mistake riding into that town; a mistake which had cost him dearly and for which he had paid a hefty price. Tom Dix wondered, as his eyes studied the people he rode past, if this too was a mistake. That last occasion had seen him sent to a penitentiary as a young man. He had come out a white-haired ghost of his former self.

He kept telling himself that this was different. He had trailed his small herd and the riders who had stolen them across the lush fertile range and through a score of valleys until he had spotted the lights of Cheyenne. The town's glowing oil-lanterns had lured him like a moth to a naked flame.

Dix had grown more and more curious as he had trailed the unseen cattle-thieves hour after hour.

He had expected them to do their brand-burning out on the open range before bringing them anywhere near the knowledgeable cattle-buyers' agents. Yet they had not done so. They had headed straight for Cheyenne with the steers bearing his and Dan's registered brand on their hides.

Why?

Why steal so few steers when there were bigger herds to be had on the millions of acres of Wyoming grasslands? Why bring them into Cheyenne before brand-burning them?

So many questions and not a single answer.

The rider wondered who these men were.

Again the nagging question filled his tired mind. Why were they wasting their time stealing his pitifully small herd when there were still vast numbers of fattened steers to be had on his neighbours' cattle spreads?

It simply did not add up.

Tom Dix eased his weight off the saddle and glanced over his shoulders at the men and women who were still filling the boardwalks to both sides of the street.

There were more people on the streets of Cheyenne during the hours of darkness than most towns could boast at high noon, he thought. The smell of stale beer and countless privies filled the night air. Music from almost every building pervaded the lantern-lit streets.

There was a haunting dirge drifting over him which had nothing to do with the pianos or guitars within the saloons and gaming-houses. It was the sound of untold numbers of cattle as they lamented in the stock-pens near the rail-tracks. It was as if they knew what fate awaited them.

Dix held his skittish mount in check as he guided it along the centre of the wide street. The sound of a locomotive whistle echoed all about him as it bounced off the brick and wooden buildings.

The man who had once been one of Texas's highest-paid gunfighters knew that he had probably bitten off more than even he could chew this time. Thoughts flashed through his mind of the seemingly endless days he had spent in a chain-gang. Dix knew that he dare not make a similar mistake here. His speed and deadly accuracy with his guns could only be used if the law was on his side.

A cold shiver traced his spine.

There was no way he could afford to be sent back to prison again. He was too old.

Tom Dix began to regret not having his partner Dan Shaw at his side. For Shaw was a retired United States marshal whose very presence ensured that other lawmen listened before they reached for their guns or a rope.

Dix continued to look around him as his horse slowly made its way along the long wide thoroughfare. Side-streets spurred off in all directions. He suddenly realized how big Cheyenne actually was.

If his twenty white-faced cattle were in this massive township, he knew that he might never find them.

He had followed the tracks all the way from his ranch to the outskirts of the town, but then the wide streets of churned-up mud had made it impossible to know who or what had travelled up and down them.

Tom Dix spotted the sheriff's office to his left. He drew his mount up alongside the raised boardwalk and stared through the windows at the blackness within the building. He bit his lip, then turned the mount away from the hitching rail and stared around the busy streets again.

Dix knew that he could do nothing without the knowledge of the local law officers. Dan Shaw had taught him that. To act alone was to risk everything.

'Ya looking for the sheriff, mister?' a man in a well-made suit asked.

Dix looked at the man.

'Yep. You any idea where he is?'

The man pulled out a watch from his vest pocket and opened its lid.

'Old Rufas is probably in the Little Dice about now.'

Dix leaned over his saddle horn.

'What's the Little Dice, friend?'

'A saloon down yonder,' the man replied. He snapped the lid of the watch shut and returned it to the silk vest-pocket. 'It is a favourite haunt of the sheriff. They got females there and the sheriff likes females.'

Tom Dix touched the brim of his Stetson.

'Much obliged, friend.'

The man watched as Dix turned his horse and headed off in the direction he had indicated. Then he continued on his way.

The Little Dice did not take a lot of finding. The sound of a well-tuned piano could have guided even a blind man to its front entrance. The sounds of men and women enjoying themselves also appeared louder than in most of the adjoining buildings. Dix eased back on his reins as he drew closer to the saloon. He looked up at the six windows above him. Lantern-light filtered through their lace drapes out into the street. Dix nodded knowingly to himself as he listened to the noises of men and women behind those drapes.

The well-dressed man outside the sherifff's office had been right. They had women here, he thought.

A half-dozen horses were tied up outside its wide red brick frontage against three hitching rails. He imagined that most of the Little Dice's patrons lived within walking distance and only the unfit or darn lazy rode to savour the fleshpots on the menu.

Dix stopped his mount and dismounted.

He looped his reins over the hitching pole and then stepped up on to the wooden boardwalk. He stood like a statue staring into the well-illuminated interior as men flowed in and out through its swing-doors.

Somewhere inside he hoped to see a sheriff's star pinned to the shirt of the town's elected lawman. The harder he looked, the less he saw. Above the heart of the busy drinking-area a carpeted staircase rose to a landing. A fancy painted balustrade had been placed to ensure that drunken patrons who walked out from the countless doors did not fall on to other unsuspecting Little Dice customers.

'Out the way, old-timer!' a burly man grunted as he shouldered the once famous gunfighter aside and proceeded out into the gloom. Dix stared at the man for a few moments, then returned his attention on the inside of the saloon. There had been a time when he would have reacted to such an unmannerly action, but that was long ago. Now he used his brains as well as his deadly skills.

Dix drew in his belly and pushed the swing-doors apart with his gloved hands. The people were crammed inside the saloon tighter than peaches in a can. He forced his way through them silently, making his way toward the unseen bar counter.

The smell of stale perfume as females in dirty dance-hall clothes brushed past him reminded Dix of days when he too lusted for the fleeting pleasures found in the arms of soiled doves. But that was also a very long time ago. A time when he had more sap in him.

He managed to reach the bar and used his still-broad shoulders to wedge his way between the drunken regulars. He used the reflections in the long well-polished mirror to try to locate the sheriff. There were so many faces and none of them looked remotely like a lawman. There were no gleaming stars pinned to the chests of anyone as far as Dix could observe.

'What'll it be?' one of the quartet of bartenders asked Dix in a raised voice as he fought above the deafening sound of men talking and women giggling.

'Where's the sheriff?' Dix replied in an equally loud tone.

The bartender leaned forward and growled: 'We

serve drinks, old man. Not give out local gossip. If ya don't wanna drink, then get the hell out of this saloon.'

Tom Dix pushed the brim of his Stetson off his brow and glared at the bartender.

'Beer!'

'Beer it is.' The man grabbed a glass and pushed it under the beer tap. As he drew the beer he stared at the face of his newest customer. 'Have I ever seen you before?'

'You ever been to prison?' Dix responded sharply.

The expression on the bartender's face altered. It was as if every drop of colour had been drained from his features in a heartbeat.

'Prison?'

Dix nodded slowly. 'Yep. You ever been in prison?'

'Nope.' The man nervously placed the glass before Dix and accepted the silver dollar. 'What was ya in prison for?'

'Murder,' Dix answered.

'Murder?' The man swallowed hard and nervously opened the cash-drawer before fumbling for change.

'Yep. I killed me a sheriff once.' Dix took a sip of the beer and then continued to stare hard at the bartender who placed the coins on top of the wet bar counter. 'Now I'll ask you again. Have you seen the sheriff?'

The eyes of the bartender darted back and forth as if searching for someone to help him or a place to hide. He was afraid and it showed.

'Ya ain't gonna kill him, are ya?'

Dix took another sip of the beer. 'Nope. But I might just end your misery if you don't give me some answers, barkeep.'

'He's upstairs having his daily . . .'

'Ya don't have to draw me no pictures.' Dix glanced up at the balcony that encircled the saloon. He had never seen so many well-used doors. He then lowered his eyes and focused hard on the sweating bartender.

'How long 'til he gets back down here?'

The bar looked up and then sighed heavily as relief rushed over him. He raised a shaking finger and pointed.

'There's old Rufas now, mister. There he is.'

Dix turned and looked to where the finger was aimed. He saw the man with a star pinned to a black-silk vest. He was about thirty-five and had a black moustache which hung limply to his upper lip. If the sheriff had a mouth, he sure hid it well, Dix thought. The lawman was smiling the way men always smile after sowing their wild oats. His hands were buckling up his gunbelt as he walked towards the top of the wide staircase.

'You sure ya ain't gonna kill him?' There was concern in the voice behind Dix's shoulder.

'If'n I did, at least the varmint would die happy.

Keep the change, sonny.' Dix finished his drink and set the empty glass down. 'Stop frettin'. I ain't gonna hurt him.'

The bartender scooped up the wet coins and dropped them into the pocket of his white apron. He watched as the tall white-haired man disappeared into the crowd.

Tom Dix reached the foot of the stairs at the same time as the satisfied sheriff stepped off the brightly coloured carpet on to the sawdust-covered floor.

Rufas Harper looked at the face before him and stopped walking. His right hand moved to the handle of his Colt as though he felt that he might have to use it.

'Back off, old man.'

'Easy, Sheriff,' Dix said. 'I ain't looking for no trouble with ya. I'm looking for help.'

Harper tilted his head back and looked hard into the face before him.

'You look like the sort of man who don't need the help of others, *amigo*.'

Dix bit his lower lip.

'I've had my herd rustled, Sheriff.'

Harper started walking once again, heading for the swing-doors and the street. Dix followed at the man's shoulder.

'You and half a dozen other ranchers around Cheyenne, old-timer. I don't even get excited any more.'

The air was cool out in the street. Both men stood on the edge of the boardwalk and allowed the light breeze to brush the smell of cigar smoke off them.

'I trailed them rustlers here,' Dix added.

'To Cheyenne?'

'Yep.'

'Then I figure that you done lost them. There must be a thousand head of steers down at the railhead. Maybe even more. Your steers are probably down there mixed in with all that other beef.' Harper shrugged as he found a cigar in his shirt pocket and bit off its tip. 'I ain't gonna waste my time looking for the critters.'

Dix watched as the lawman ran a match down a wooden upright and shielded its flame with his large hands. Smoke billowed from his mouth.

'You're the law and I want you to help me find them.'

Sheriff Harper rubbed his chin thoughtfully.

'Once them brand-burners have altered the brands, there ain't no chance of finding the animals.'

'They ain't had a chance to burn my brand off my herd, Sheriff.' Dix said. 'I've been on their tail since dawn. I trailed them here and my cattle are somewhere in Cheyenne with my brand still on them.'

'How many were there?'

'Twenty,' Dix replied.

Harper laughed.

'Twenty? Are you joshing me?'

'What's so funny, Sheriff?'

'You want me to look for twenty cattle in a town filled with who knows how many steers?' Rufas Harper looked at the face of the confused older man. 'Go home, mister. Go home.'

'Not until I get my herd back,' Dix said. 'Me and my partner have worked hard trying to create a herd. Now all our work has been stolen. There might only be twenty of them, but this time next year there would be more than double that figure.'

Harper looked unconcerned as he puffed on his cigar and looked around the busy street.

'I don't understand why you're so excited. Twenty steers ain't worth nothing. Not in this town.'

Tom Dix stepped down into the street and untied his reins from the hitching rail.

'Reckon I better try and handle this myself then, Sheriff.'

'Don't go breakin' the law, old-timer,' Rufas Harper warned Dix as he stepped into his stirrup and rose atop his quarter horse. 'Coz if you go killing somebody, I'll have to throw the book at ya. Understand?'

Tom Dix gathered up his reins and looked hard at the face before him. He sighed heavily in disappointment.

'Don't you go fretting about me, Sheriff. I'm just

gonna go and get my steers back. If'n someone draws on me, I'll shoot back.'

'What's ya name?'

'Tom Dix.'

Harper tapped the ash off his smoke. 'I heard about you. You're a convicted killer, ain't ya? You shot a sheriff down South, as I recall.'

Dix held his horse in check. 'I served my time. Twelve years to be exact.'

'I'd have strung ya up!' Harper spat.

'Reckon so!' Dix nodded. 'But I was convicted by a jury and I served my time.'

'That's as maybe but I don't cotton to killers wandering around in my town, Dix. You even sneeze and I'll come looking for ya with a rope.'

'Could ya look for my cattle as well, Sheriff?' Tom Dix raised an eyebrow.

'Ya got a smart mouth, Dix. I don't cotton to folks with smart mouths.'

Tom Dix said nothing. He turned the head of his horse and spurred.

Harper continued to puff on his cigar as the quarter horse leapt into action. The rider galloped down the street in the direction of the railyards. A man wandered up to the Little Dice saloon and stepped on to the boardwalk beside the brooding lawman.

'Seth,' Harper acknowledged.

'What's wrong, Rufas?'

'Got me a murderer wanderin' around my town,

Seth. A large as life sheriff-killer.'

Seth squinted hard at the rider.

'What ya gonna do, Rufas?'

'Go get my horse, Seth,' Harper replied.

THREE

Lightning forked out across the heavens above the busy town as Tom Dix drew in his reins and stopped the exhausted mount. The smell had guided the horseman through the maze of twisting streets straight to the scores of cattle-pens. His gloved hands expertly held the horse in check as he stared in disbelief at the acres of wooden fence-poles lit up by countless oil-lanterns.

He had never imagined there could be so many penned cattle in any one place at any one time. An ear-splitting train whistle drew his attention.

A startled Tom Dix looked up. His eyes narrowed.

Smoke billowed from the stack of a stationary locomotive, sending sparks cascading into the air, whilst teams of men worked feverishly filling its freight cars with the wide-eyed beasts.

Dix was uneasy. He began to understand why the sheriff had not bothered to come here.

Suddenly the sky lit up. The flashes of lightning came only a few seconds before the rumbling above him. His horse was skittish and required every ounce of his strength to control, but Dix was equal to it.

Rain began to fall. It slowly started to wash the trail dust from the tired rider and his mount.

The white faces of the nervous cattle appeared like ghosts as the eerie blue light traced above the cattle-pens. It was as if even the elements were against the lone horseman. Tom Dix knew that if the massive beasts could leap over the four-post pens, they would.

Their wailing had a desperation about it that chilled him.

For the first time since he had set out from his distant ranch, Tom Dix realized the true magnitude of what faced him.

Rufas Harper had been right.

There was little hope that he would be able find his twenty cattle amid so many other identical steers.

It would be easier finding a needle in a haystack.

Tom Dix shook his head and was about to turn his mount when he heard something on the other side of the tracks far beyond the steaming train.

He stood in his stirrups and allowed the horse to walk through the driving rain in the direction of the noise which had alerted him that there were other people around the stock pens.

The quarter horse responded to every slight movement of its master's gloved hands as it walked nervously along the narrow gaps between the cattle-pens toward the cattle-trucks.

As Dix tapped his spurs, his mount walked tentatively over the gleaming metal lines. The rider pulled his collar up against the driving rain and stared at the unexpected sight before him.

There were four sets of railtracks laid out next to each other on the wet ground. There were even more stock-pens and scores of wooden buildings fringing the tracks. Another steaming locomotive stood with its cars empty on the furthest set of tracks.

The storm above him was growing angrier with every heartbeat that pounded inside the veteran horseman's chest. Yet Dix seemed unaware of anything except his curiosity at finding whatever it was which had made the noise that had lured him across the massive stockyards.

Again he heard the strange sound and tried to see through the rain, which continued to fall with ever more ferocity. It was futile. All he could do was keep his mount walking and pray that the rain would ease up long enough for him to be able to see clearly.

Then his prayers were answered. The rain eased as the wind changed direction.

Lightning forked down in the distance and struck an unsuspecting tree. The sound of the explosion echoed all around Cheyenne but that was not the noise which had drawn Dix to this place.

His eyes darted all around him.

There was a desperation in his search as he controlled the quarter horse beneath him.

Then he spotted something a hundred yards away just inside the open doors of a large black building.

The glowing of a well-shielded fire a few feet inside the open doors of the building illuminated nine men moving around its vast interior. They were working feverishly.

Dix's eyes narrowed until he no longer saw the rain between himself and the building, but were focused solely on the men ahead of him. He could see the long branding-irons in their hands and smell the unmistakable aroma of burning.

Then he spotted the steers behind the men.

Were they his small herd?

Tom Dix turned his horse's head and made towards the large building.

With every stride of his mount's long legs, he knew that he was riding towards trouble.

Had he located the brand-burners?

FOUR

The storm was now directly overhead. The horseman knew that if one of those white lightning-bolts snaked down from the sky and found him atop his horse, he would never discover anything about the men with the branding-irons. All he would find out was whether his name was on Saint Peter's guest list or whether he had an appointment in a much hotter place. Neither option appealed to him. Tom Dix threw his right leg over his mount's neck and slid off the saddle. Before his boots had landed in the mud, he had drawn both his prized Colts.

Dix gently slapped the rear of his quarter horse and then crouched and ran into the dark shadows to the side of the tall building. He watched his horse continue on past the large open doorway, then he moved into the blackness towards the rear.

This was some sort of barn or warehouse, he thought. A place that was seldom used. Ideal for the brand-burners to ply their trade unknown to the railroad company. Dix held both his guns in his gloved hands as his eyes searched for a way in. Then he spotted the light escaping from around the frame of a door. Dix peered through a knot-hole in the wooden wall and watched the men carefully.

He could hear the voices inside become raised when they saw the riderless horse pass them. All nine of them moved from the hot fire to get a better look at the bedraggled horse.

That was what Dix had hoped they would do.

A few moments of distraction.

Tom Dix pushed the barrel of the Colt in his left hand into the gap between the door and its frame. He twisted the gun, levered the door open and stared in through the inch-wide opening.

His eyes focused keenly over the backs of the cattle. He counted nine men again. The thought traced through his mind once more as to why so many men would bother to steal his meagre twenty head of white-faced steers?

How much could they be worth? Hardly enough to keep these men in whiskey for a week. Yet there had to be something behind this that he had yet to fathom. Some greater purpose which he would have to try and discover, if he managed to live long enough, that was.

Dix used every shadow within the large wooden building to his advantage as he moved carefully between his uneasy livestock.

His eyes moved away from the confused men who were standing in the rain looking at his horse wandering aimlessly along the muddy ground. He looked at the cattle around him more intently.

They were definitely his, he confirmed.

He'd found his herd.

Even in the flickering light of the fire and the two oil-lamps hung on the wooden walls, he could make out his and Dan Shaw's registered brand on the hides of the beasts closest to him. Three of the other cattle had been moved away from the bulk of his herd. He could smell the smouldering of burned hide drifting off them as he edged around the large building.

The brands on the trio of steers to his right had been altered so skilfully that even though he knew they belonged to him, he could not see any errors in the brand-burners' work. These men had known exactly what they were doing with their branding irons, he thought. To brand a full grown steer was hard enough but to alter one brand into another took manpower. Dix suddenly knew why there were so many of them. It probably took at least five of the rustlers just to get the massive beasts down and hold them on the ground as another kept the fire hot with hand-bellows. Then there was the man or men with the irons. They had to get it right first time because there was no second chance when you burned into the hide of cattle. One error made the steer valueless.

No wonder there were so many of them, he thought.

Dix focused hard on the altered brands and wondered who they were registered to. Someone owned the strange mark that had been burned into the brown coats of his cattle.

But who?

Dix slowly made his way in between the seventeen large steers. With every step, he never once took his eyes off the men near the open doorway.

His mouth went suddenly dry as he realized what he might face in the next few moments.

Dix pulled the hammers back on his guns with his thumbs until they fully locked.

'It was just a horse, Larry,' Mac Mason said in a tone which gave no clue that he was the leader of the brand-burners.

Larry Brady shook his head.

'A saddle horse with no rider?'

Three of the other men, Cal Smith, Dave Travis and Toby Dwayne exhaled as one man and looked at Mason.

'Where ya reckon his rider is, Mac?' Smith asked.

Travis stepped forward. 'That's a darn good quarter horse to be roaming around without anyone in its saddle, Mac.'

Mason tilted his head and looked all around the muddy area as if trying to locate the phantom master of the loose horse. The driving rain burned into his eyes.

'Who gives a damn? Probably just a drunk cowpoke who done fell off the critter,' Mason guessed.

'Ya reckon?' Dwayne shook his head.

Another of the brand-burners, named Jeb Olsen, spat a lump of black goo to the ground and then pulled out a block of chewing-tobacco from his shirt-pocket. He bit off a chunk and then passed the tobacco to his cohorts.

'We gotta be careful, Mac. There was an *hombre* trailing us all day. That could be his nag.'

A muscular man called Sam Canute nodded in agreement.

'Jeb's right. We was trailed all day by that darn rancher.'

'We shook him off hours back.' Mason snorted as the tobacco reached him at last. He sank his teeth into it and rotated it in his mouth until it was soft enough for his teeth to chew. 'Don't you boys start gettin' scared on me. We got to finish them steers off before the train cuts out.'

Toby Dwayne was still not convinced.

'I still ain't worked out why we are wasting our time rustling a handful of steers like this when there are whole ranges full of the damn things just waiting for someone to pluck 'em like daisies.'

Mac Mason rubbed the mixture of rain and spittle off his chin with the back of his jacket-sleeve.

He stared hard at the men he had hand-picked less than six months earlier. He knew the answer to the question but was not going to let them know.

'Ya follows my orders and that's that!'

The oldest of the bunch was a thin whisper of a man named Eli Payne. He held a coiled rope in his right hand and was the finest exponent of roping in Wyoming. Payne had learned his skills long ago as a cowboy until he got tired of hard work and low pay.

'I figure that varmint on our trail was Tom Dix, Mac,' Eli said knowingly.

'Who the hell is Tom Dix?'

'He's one of the ranchers who owns these steers, Mac,' Eli explained. 'But I knows him from way back in Texas. He was a hired gunfighter in them days. There weren't no faster man with a sixgun than Tom Dix.'

'I reckon ya loco, Eli,' Jeb Olsen sneered. 'Anyways, what would a gunfighter be doin' on a cattle ranch in the middle of no place?'

'Can't be the same man. That was years back.' Mac spat. 'Anyways, I heard that Tom Dix was dead. Shot up years back on a riverboat or somethin' like that.'

Eli Payne shook the rain off his hat.

'Ya wrong. Dix went to the pen for killing a lawman down South, Mac. Must have spent more than ten years locked up before they let him go. I heard tales that he rides with a retired lawman.

Tom Dix ain't dead. He's alive and that was him on our trail all day. I'd bet my saddle on it.'

'I still say ya loco, Eli,' Olsen repeated. 'Ya never did have the guts for this kinda work. Ya seeing things coz ya just plain yella.'

There was no let-up in the rain that fell over Cheyenne as lightning streaked across the heavens above the railhead. There was a lot of night left for the brand-burners to complete their work, but none of them felt as confident as he had before setting eyes upon the riderless mount. Now there was a question-mark hanging over them. One that they seemed unable to either face or understand.

Was that Tom Dix's horse or not?

'I seen Tom Dix in the old days. I tell ya that man on our tail was him,' Eli Payne insisted.

'You sure?' Dave Travis asked.

'Yep. I know him. He rides a certain way. Tilts to his left in the saddle.' Eli Payne was uneasy. 'That was him for sure and that's his horse. He ain't the sort to go stealing from.'

'Hush up,' Mason ordered firmly.

Pete Walker shook his head. 'I ain't in this to get myself shot up by no gunslinger. I reckon we ought to high-tail it out of this town before this Dix character shows up.'

'I reckon he's already showed up, Pete,' Eli Payne said in a fearful tone that drew every eye to him. 'If he is, he'll not rest until he's put us all in Boot Hill.'

'They got law here in Cheyenne, Eli.' Sam Canute spat. 'Folks like this Dix critter can't just come in with his guns blazing or he'll be in worse trouble than us.'

Payne toyed with his trusty rope.

'Dix has a habit of killing the law when it suits him.'

There was a silence which went around the group of bedraggled rustlers. Mac Mason stepped closer to his men and clenched both his fists angrily.

'Listen to ya all. Like a bunch of women. Tom Dix must be a hundred years old by now,' Mason raged out loud. 'My white-haired mother could probably draw down on him nowadays. He probably fell off his horse back on the trail. There ain't a gunfighter alive who ain't got his equal somewhere down the trail. As soon as them white hairs start showing, it's only a matter of time before he gets himself bettered. Right?'

The brand-burners laughed.

All except one.

Eli Payne knew better than to laugh at anyone as dangerous as Tom Dix. He was the sort you touched the brim of your hat to just in case he drew his famed Colts. Eli looked hard at the soaked horse fifty yards from them. It had stopped close to the locomotive as if waiting for its master.

'Ya better be right, Mac,' Eli warned. 'Coz if ya ain't, we'll all be headed for Boot Hill.'

Mason waved a branding-iron at his men and began to usher them back into the large smoke-filled building.

'C'mon, boys. Don't listen to the old fool. We got us some work to finish before they get a full head of steam in that train's boiler.'

The men returned into the building and hastily got on with their work. All except Eli Payne. He took his time walking back.

Payne knew that Mac Mason was wrong to underestimate the legendary Tom Dix.

At least a dozen men had done so in the past and they were all dead.

FIVE

The storm was growing more ferocious with every passing second that ticked by on the golden hunter-watch tucked into the vest-pocket of the once infamous gunfighter. Tom Dix remained exactly where he was at the heart of the group of massive steers that he had raised and watched the men getting on with their jobs. It seemed that there were only a few seconds between the deafening thunderclaps above the tall wooden building and the terrifying flashes of lightning which lit up the glistening locomotives.

'C'mon, Eli!' Mason shouted at the man with the rope who continued staring out of the large wooden doors at Dix's defiant horse. 'Cut out another steer. We got to get this job done.'

Payne glanced at the furious Mason.

'Our horses are goin' loco out there, Mac.'

'Don't fret yourself. We tied 'em up good and they ain't gonna break free,' Mason growled.

Eli Payne walked to the side of the bigger, younger man and looked him in the eyes.

'But Tom Dix's horse ain't movin' a muscle out there. You ever seen a horse that lightning can't spook?'

Mason angrily grabbed his shoulders and pushed him towards the white-faced cattle with all his strength.

'Use ya rope and cut out a steer for the boys, Eli,' Mason screamed.

Eli Payne staggered across the hay-covered floor but regained his balance when faced by the seventeen cattle they had sectioned off in the corner of the large building. He sighed heavily and started to uncoil his rope.

When he looked up at the massive beasts, he suddenly saw the face of the man he had been talking about.

Tom Dix was staring straight at him.

Even the white hair and wrinkled features could not take away a single ounce of the power which had made Dix feared throughout the West a dozen years earlier.

Eli Payne felt as if his high-heeled boots had been nailed to the ground. All he could do was stare at the vision before him, standing amid the white-faced steers. Payne's eyes lowered until he saw the pair of cocked Colts in the gloved hands of the motionless man.

Payne's eyes widened.

The rope dropped from his skilled hands as he felt himself shaking.

'Now what's wrong, Eli?' Mason called out.

Sweat traced down the features of the terrified man.

'He's havin' a fit or somethin', Mac.' Toby Dwayne spat as he dropped some branding-irons into the fire.

Mason marched to Payne's side, grabbed his shoulder and swung the shaking man around.

Suddenly a flash of blinding light filled the interior of the large building. Payne sank to his knees.

'What's wrong with ya?' Mason shouted above the sound of a massive thunderclap.

'Tom Dix!' Payne mumbled fearfully.

'What about him?' Mason yelled.

Eli Payne looked up at Mason's face. Mason had never seen so much terror etched in anyone's features before.

'He's here! He's here!'

Mason released his grip and looked in the direction of the moaning cattle.

'What's wrong, Mac?' Cal Smith asked as he walked up to Mason's side.

'Dix is in here!' Mason drew both his guns from their holsters.

Now it was his turn for fear to fill every sinew of his being. He screwed his eyes up and squinted hard into the dark shadows that filled the back of the wooden building.

The brand-burners dropped their irons and hauled an array of guns from their holsters. Each of them edged their way towards their leader. These were not men who were used to facing their enemies head on. They were thieves who only used their weapons on the innocent or the backs of better men.

The guns shook in the hands of the men who flanked Mason on both sides. Only Mason himself seemed capable of holding his Colts in unshaking hands.

'Where is he?'

'Ya sure he's there, Mac?'

'Let's high-tail it!'

Mac Mason heard nothing except the violent explosions which shook the dust from the wooden rafters above him. He cautiously moved forward and chewed on the plug of tobacco in his dry mouth.

He wanted to spit the bitter juice from his mouth but knew that to do so could give a man such as Tom Dix the advantage all such gunfighters required.

With his heart pounding inside his massive chest, Mason stepped closer and closer to the nervous cattle. His eyes darted all around the black shadows, searching for the man he had tried to dismiss as nothing more than a figment of Eli Payne's vivid imagination.

'Come on out, Dix!' Mason heard himself growl

as he pushed the heads of the steers away with the cold-blue steel barrels of his guns. 'Come out and face us, ya bastard.'

The steers continued to moan but he could not see anyone.

Mason paused in his advance.

'Keep lookin', boys. He has to be in here some place unless old Eli was seeing things again.'

The rustlers fanned out to both sides of the wooden building with their pistols held out before them. Each of them had exactly the same thought as they followed the instructions of their gruff leader: if Tom Dix was inside this structure, they would find him and open fire.

Suddenly there was a noise to Mason's right. A scurrying sound that drew every gun barrel towards it within an instant.

A startled rat raced from a mound of hay and ran straight at the men.

Cal Smith fanned his gun hammer vainly at the rodent.

The bullets tore through the wooden walls, allowing shafts of lantern-light to filter in. Mac Mason turned and screamed at the men behind him.

'Ya get him?'

There was another long silence before Larry Brady coughed and started to speak.

'It was just a rat, Mac. Cal got spooked.'

Mason's eyes narrowed.

'Damn fool!'

Then another noise caught their attention. Mason twisted on his heels, then crouched. With his guns at hip-level he made his way through the nervous steers. Then he saw the rear door of the building bouncing against its wooden frame.

Mason rose to his full height and forced his way back to his confused men.

'He's outside! We got him running scared!'

Mason's eight followers went towards the large open door. Then they were stopped in their tracks by the low drawl of the man they sought coming from above them. Their eyes gazed up into the shadows and saw the haunting image of the veteran gunfighter with his guns aimed down at them.

'I ain't gone nowhere, *amigo*!' Dix corrected as he stood on the platform between a half-dozen bales of hay.

'I told ya it was Tom Dix!' Eli Payne scrambled to his feet and looked up to the high loft. He raised his hands in passive submission when he focused on Dix at the top of the wooden ladder.

'Drop them hoglegs, boys!' Dix ordered.

Mac Mason squinted at the figure above them and then spat a lump of well-chewed tobacco at the ground.

'Don't listen to him, men. He's just an old man.'

Tom Dix stepped to the very edge of the loft floor and cocked the hammers of his guns until they locked fully into position.

'Ya listen to him and I'll kill all of you,' he warned the brand-burners.

One by one the men dropped their guns on to the soft ground. Mason turned his head and spat again. This time it was at the feet of his own hired hands. He could not hide the disgust he felt.

'Ya yella swine!' Mason snarled.

Cal Smith dropped his Colt and raised his arms high.

'I ain't gonna try and pull on him, Mac. I might be dumb but I ain't that dumb.'

'Ya scared of an old-timer? We can take him.' Mac Mason could not understand how others did not share his own conviction.

More of the rustlers dropped their weapons.

'You heard me. Drop them guns,' Tom Dix shouted down at Mason. 'I'm serious. Dead serious.'

The words had barely left the gunfighter's lips when Mason squeezed the triggers. Two white-hot fountains of venom were unleashed from the barrels of the rustler's guns. Dix felt the heat of the bullets as they passed within inches of him.

Gunsmoke masked the rustlers as Dix returned fire.

Suddenly it was as if the sky itself had exploded directly above the big building. The noise and the blinding light came at exactly the same time. The entire structure rocked on its foundations. The wooden shingles above Tom Dix's head shattered as a fork of lightning punched its way through the roof.

Lethal bolts of blue-and-white electricity cascaded in every direction over the stunned Dix.

The cattle below him suddenly broke loose and stampeded towards the open doorway and the rustlers. The men threw themselves in all directions as the terrified steers charged blindly towards the open doorway.

Another twisting arrow of electrical fury lit up the interior of the building as it destroyed everything in its path. The light was blinding to every one of the men within the heart of the creaking edifice. Bales of hay ignited all around Dix.

He felt the heat of the lightning-bolt pass across the back of his jacket. Only the rain prevented the gunfighter from being engulfed in flames.

Flames leapt heavenward from every corner as Dix holstered his weapons and went to reach for the ladder. The entire frame of the building seemed to move as if pushed by the hand of an invisible giant. Dix stumbled and felt the solid wooden platform beneath his cowboy boots give way.

Desperately his gloved hands searched for the ladder when angry flames engulfed it and forced him back.

Then another shaft of vicious lightning came crashing through a different part of the roof. This time Dix saw it coming and tried to move away.

It was too late. There was nowhere to go on the creaking platform. It began to tilt as its support beam fell to the ground.

Dix knew that only a few nails were holding what was left of the loft in place. Nails which were slowly being prised free under the sheer weight of the unsupported platform.

Then a massive wooden joist crashed down from above Dix and caught him across his wide shoulders. The impact took every breath of wind from him. Dix was thrown like a rag-doll helplessly into the billowing smoke which rose up from below his high vantage point.

Tom Dix hit the ground hard. A million red-hot burning splinters showered over his still body as the building collapsed in flames all around him.

SIX

The burning embers which covered his entire length felt like a hundred spiders gnawing into his bruised and battered body. Dix had no way of knowing that his jeans and jacket were alight as he lay stunned on the floor of the disintegrating building. At last his head cleared enough for him to open his eyes. He tried to move but there was something holding him down. Dix pushed at the the churned-up mud until his face lifted a few inches off its surface. He tried to suck in some of the air that had been knocked out of his lungs when he landed heavily on the ground.

Dix tilted his head, glanced at his legs and saw the massive joist pinning him to the spot. Then his sore eyes widened when he realized that flames were licking across its entire twenty-foot length. Droplets of fire dripped like liquid over his trapped lower half as old paint melted on the wooden joist.

Dix clawed desperately at the ground in a vain attempt to escape, but he could not move an inch. His eyes glanced upward and saw what was left of the high wooden walls. Massive chunks of blackened wood began to fall all around him.

Then, when Dix thought that all was lost, he heard raised voices and felt powerful fingers and strong hands grabbing at him. Men whom he had never even met before were risking their lives to save his. There was a sudden relief as the weight was kicked off his legs. He felt the anxious men dragging him out of the inferno at breakneck speed.

They rolled Dix across the wet muddy ground until they were satisfied that they had extinguished every last burning fragment of his clothing. Dix wiped the mud from his eyes with gloved fingers just in time to see one of the blazing walls collapse across the very spot where he had been lying only seconds earlier. Dix swallowed hard as it dawned on him how close an escape it had been.

'He's OK. He's OK,' a huge railroad worker announced to his companions.

'Pity the building ain't OK, Ray,' another well-built man added. 'Look at it.'

The man with arms like tree-trunks, named Ray, tutted and shook his head.

'That'll make the bosses a mite ornery, Hector.'

Tom Dix pushed himself up and somehow managed to get to his feet. He staggered to the side of one of his saviours and felt the man's powerful hand slip under his arm.

'Thanks, friend.' Dix coughed.

'Weren't nothing, old-timer,' the burly figure said. 'Me and Hector couldn't let ya fry in there, could we.'

Hector nodded in agreement. 'Ray is correct. Besides the smell of burned person is something awful.'

'Well, it meant a lot to me.' Dix straightened up and looked as the last of the burning wooden framework collapsed. It was like a million fireflies rising up into the air. Even the rain could not stop the fire's final defiance.

It had reduced the huge structure to little more than ashes in less than ten minutes.

'What was you doin' in there, mister?' the man asked as Dix tried to regain his balance.

'There was a bunch of brand-burners in there and I went in to try and stop them altering the brands on my steers,' Dix answered weakly. 'Then lightning hit the darn place and it went up like a tinder box.'

Ray nodded as he rubbed his tattooed arms. 'That must have been the varmints we saw high-tailing it out of town when we come to try and put out the fire.'

Dix exhaled and coughed again.

'So they got away, huh?'

'Yep.'

'Have ya seen about twenty white-faced steers running around here? Tom Dix was now able to support his weight. He walked closer to the smouldering timbers.

'Don't fret. The boys will round them up for ya,' the larger man gruffed knowingly. 'Ain't that right, Hector?'

'Sure enough, Ray,' Hector agreed.

Tom Dix was caked in mud but the continuous rain was slowly washing it off what was left of his trail clothes. Then the hoofbeats of two riders drew Dix's attention as their mounts negotiated the railtracks behind him. He turned and saw Sheriff Harper and Seth Green reining in a few yards behind him. The lawman dismounted and tossed his reins into the hands of his deputy.

'What in tarnation have you been doin' here, Dix?' Harper yelled at the bedraggled figure. 'I warned ya not to start no trouble in Cheyenne, didn't I?'

'You told me not to kill nobody, Sheriff,' Dix retorted. 'I ain't killed nobody.'

Harper raised his voice even louder.

'But ya burned down that railroad warehouse, didn't ya?'

'Nope. I did not!' Dix insisted.

'Then who did?'

Tom Dix stared hard into the eyes of the angry sheriff.

'It was struck by lightning and I almost got

myself roasted alive.'

Sheriff Harper gritted his teeth. 'What was ya doing in there anyways?'

'I done your job for ya. I tracked them brand-burners to that damn barn or whatever it was, and got the drop on them.' Dix fumed. 'Then the damn place got hit by the darndest chunk of lightning I ever done saw. The hay bales up in the loft caught fire and them rustling *hombres* escaped.'

Rufas Harper wiped the rain from his face.

'Are you still jabbering on about rustlers, old-timer? I'm starting to think that you're plumb loco. Where are these brand-burners now?'

'They high-tailed it.' Dix sighed.

'Are you sure that you ain't having visions, Dix? Seeing things that no sane varmint can see?'

The big railroad-worker named Ray stepped forward and folded his muscular arms.

'Me and Hector saw them brand-burners, Sheriff.'

Harper glanced at the big man. 'You and Hector saw a bunch of riders galloping off. That's all. How do ya know they were brand-burners, Ray?'

'But what else could they be?'

'Riders! They might just have been a bunch of riders!' The lawman snorted. 'Just coz Tom Dix says they're rustlers don't make it so.'

Dix clenched his fists and was just about to hit Harper when he spied a rider coming through the driving rain towards them. He walked away from the men and rested his gloved knuckles on his gun grips. He squinted against the rain and watched as Dan Shaw slowly approached.

'About time you got here, Dan!'

Dan Shaw eased his tall black mount to a halt and studied the scene before looking down on his partner.

'It took a while for me to figure that you and the stock was gone, Dixie. But I'm here now.'

Tom Dix nodded. 'Could be you just went back to bed after doin' ya chores.'

'I let you out of my sight for five minutes and look what happens. Damn, you're a mess.'

Dix felt a smile trace his bruised face.

'Our steers were rustled and I trailed them here, Dan. I almost had the *hombres* that done it when . . .'

'How come your clothes are smokin', Dixie?' Dan Shaw dismounted and led his horse across the muddy ground towards the remains of the fire. 'You weren't in there were you?'

'Yep. Darn place got hit by lightning and caught fire.'

'Lightning, huh?'

'Yep. A whole wagonful of lightning, Dan.'

Rufas Harper cleared his throat. 'I ain't finished with you, Dix. Get ya scrawny hide back here.'

Dan Shaw turned and looked at Harper.

'Lucky for you I showed up, Sheriff.'

'What ya mean?' Harper asked. 'Who are ya anyways?'

'The name's Dan Shaw. I could hear ya shoutin' at Dixie here before I crossed them railtracks,' Dan answered. 'Like I said, it was lucky for you that I showed up when I did. Dixie has got quite a temper on him, sonny.'

'Another old man with a smart mouth that don't know when to quit.' Rufas Harper snorted. 'I ought to throw the pair of ya in jail for disturbing the peace.'

'I'm an old man who was a United States marshal up until a year back, sonny,' Dan informed the younger man. 'But Dixie here is faster with his guns now than he was when I first met him. Like I said, it's lucky for you that I showed up when I did. I just might have saved you from having ya ears pierced.'

Harper pointed at the two men before him. His finger was shaking in a mixture of fear and anger.

'How can a retired lawman be friends with a no-good sheriff-killer?'

Dan Shaw walked up to Harper and forcibly brushed his arm aside. He stood toe to toe with the younger man.

'If'n you knew Dixie like I do, you'd not be so quick to judge him. Now I reckon it's time you went back to wherever it is you picked up that stink of cheap perfume, Sheriff. Me and my friend have got us work to do.'

'You might be pushin' ya luck, old-timer,' Rufas Harper growled.

'I don't reckon so, Sheriff,' Dan drawled. 'But if you are hankering to test your theory, go ahead. I ain't lived this long by not being able to use this gun.'

'I still say there ain't no brand-burners in Cheyenne,' said the sheriff.

'Not now they've run off,' Dan agreed sternly.

Harper backed off, then accepted his reins from Green and mounted his horse. He swung the head of the soaked creature around and spurred hard.

The small gathering watched the two horses make their way over the shining railtracks and disappear behind the locomotive and its heavily laden freight-cars.

'Gee, Dan. I never seen you so all-fired up before,' Dix said humbly. 'I was starting to get worried you might draw that gun of yours.'

Dan Shaw turned and looked at his friend.

'Darn it, Dixie. How can you smile when half ya clothes have been burned off your back?'

'It ain't easy, old-timer.'

Dan Shaw pulled on his reins and led his tall black horse towards his partner, a man whom Shaw felt obliged to look after even though there was no reason apart from his being the lawman who had brought him to justice more than a dozen years earlier. Dan Shaw had known then that it had been an accident that had cost Dix twelve years of his freedom. He had seen a young Tom Dix being taken to prison and an old man who had eventually staggered back out of the gates. Guilt had weighed heavily on the shoulders of the retired lawman ever since. Yet the friendship between the two men had grown even stronger over those years.

Theirs was a bond of mutual respect, forged in an iron that was stronger than anything a blacksmith could fashion on his anvil.

As the two men walked together towards Dix's waiting quarter horse the rain stopped.

'Lost your hat, I see,' Dan noted.

Dix looked at the holes in his clothes.

'I can buy a new hat and clothes. But I almost lost everything else, Dan.'

The two men reached the sodden horse and Dix picked up his reins from the ground. He looped them over the head of his trusty mount.

'When them wranglers round up our steers we can head on back to the ranch,' said Dan.

Tom Dix stopped and looked at his pal.

'I ain't going nowhere until we bring them brand-burners to book, Dan. Somebody in Cheyenne has to stop them varmints from ruining folks' lives.'

Dan Shaw smiled.

'I knew you'd say that, old friend.'

Dix stepped into his stirrup and carefully hoisted himself atop his horse.

'Reckon you're a bad influence on a weathered old gunslinger, Dan.' He laughed.

Shaw nodded and turned the head of his black horse until it was aimed back at the sprawling town.

'Yep,' Dan agreed as he urged his mount to start walking beside the quarter horse. 'But I reckon we ought to buy you some new duds and then get us a room for the night before we do any sniffing around Cheyenne.'

'Hey, Dan. Do you reckon I need a bath?' Dix asked.

Dan Shaw shrugged. 'If you're willing to try something new, Dixie. I ain't gonna stop you.'

SEVEN

Sheriff Harper had barely placed his head upon the pillow when he heard the door of his office being hammered until its glass started to shake. Against his better judgement, he got off his bed and dragged on his pants. He staggered down from the two-room quarters above the office and walked barefoot to the door. He raised the blind and then stared at the telegrapher.

'What ya want?' Harper shouted.

The small man held the scrap of paper in his hand.

'This is important, Rufas. Open up.'

Harper turned the key and then pulled the door towards him. He grabbed the paper from the hand of the telegraph-worker and unfolded it.

'This better be good,' the sheriff warned. 'I've been up all night doing my duty.'

The man nodded knowingly. 'Sure ya have,

Rufas. The Little Dice saloon must wear you out.'

Harper's expression altered as the words slowly sank in to his weary brain.

'Hush up. So I've got me a very important visitor coming in on the noon train, huh?'

'That's what it says.'

'Get lost. You're annoying me.' Sheriff Harper slammed the door in the face of the smiling man and read the wire again. It was signed simply 'a friend'. Rufas Harper knew a lot of folks in various towns along the railtracks. But none he would have regarded as a friend.

'What in tarnation does this mean?' Harper asked himself aloud. 'I've got a very important visitor arriving by the noon train. Who could that be? And what does the varmint have to do with me?'

He glanced at the large clock on the far wall of his office. It was 10.30.

'Damn! I reckon I'd better get myself dressed and go see who this critter is.' Harper screwed the scrap of paper up in his hand and tossed it on to his desk.

There was a noise out in the foyer of the Cheyenne Hotel which drew the attention of every one within its lavish interior. It was the sound of a man entering from the street. A man whose entire body hurt. Dan Shaw looked up from his half-eaten ham and eggs. He hardly recognized the figure of Tom Dix when the veteran gunfighter walked tentatively into the hotel dining-room in his new clothes.

It was obvious from the expression on Dix's face that he was still in considerable pain. He sat down next to his partner, removed his new hat and placed it on the empty chair next to him. He looked at his pal.

'Darn it.'

'You OK, Dixie?' Shaw asked.

The gunfighter's wrinkled eyes glanced across to his friend. He forced a smile, then rested his arms on the table and toyed with the shining cutlery.

'Reckon that bath I had last night made my burns a tad angry, Dan. These new clothes seem to be rubbing what's left of my hide off as well.'

'You look darn pretty.' Shaw grinned.

'Funny.' Dix tried to find a way of sitting on the hard chair which did not rub his blistered skin. It was impossible.

'Nice footwear.' Dan pointed his fork at the polished black high-heeled boots.

Dix nodded.

'Yep. The trouble is they hurt like crazy.'

'You should have bought the right size.'

'I did. The trouble is my feet are swollen up due to the fire burning my old boots half off.' Dix signalled to the waitress and pointed at his friend's meal. He wanted the same. 'Reckon I'll be OK when all the blisters burst.'

'I'm trying to eat here, Dixie. Don't start going into detail about your injuries until I've finished.'

Dix smiled.

'The doc said that he'd never seen so much skin burned off a man before.'

Dan Shaw lifted the coffee pot and poured his friend a cup of the black beverage. He watched silently as Dix used a soup-spoon to get as much sugar into the cup as possible.

'You got enough sugar there, Dixie?'

Dix used the handle of the spoon to stir the coffee and looked at his smiling partner.

'We don't see quality sugar often enough, Dan. I figure I ought to try and get me enough to tide me over until the next time.'

'Sam and Hector came over here earlier and said that the railroad wranglers had managed to catch our twenty steers and herd them into an empty pen down near the tracks. They said that three of them had been rebranded by them rustlers.' Dan used a slice of bread to mop up what was left of his meal.

'That's fine,' Dix said sipping at the sweet drink.

'I thought you'd be happy.' Dan pushed his plate away from him and waved at the waitress. 'You can bring the pie now, honey. Pour some cream over it.'

The waitress smiled politely.

Tom Dix lowered the cup from his lips and gazed into what was left of the black coffee.

'Hold on a tad. Three of our white-faced had their brands changed. Yeah?'

'What you thinking about, Dixie?' Shaw asked curiously.

'Three had been rebranded.' Tom Dix muttered into the cup again.

'Yeah. I know. I just told you that.' Shaw watched the handsome young waitress move across the room in their direction with a tray in her hands. She placed the plate of ham and eggs in front of his friend and then a bowl with a large slice of apple-pie covered in cream before him.

'Thanks, dear.'

'You're welcome.' The female smiled and returned to the aromatic kitchens.

Dix looked at his pal and raised an eyebrow. 'Honey? Dear? You be careful there, old-timer.'

Shaw blushed as he picked up his spoon and sank it into the pie.

'Hush up, Dixie. I was just being friendly.'

'What's her name, Dan?' Dix asked.

'Susan,' Shaw replied.

'You old fool.' Dix cut up his bacon and popped a forkful into his mouth. 'You're probably older than her pa.'

Dan Shaw cleared his throat.

'What's so interesting about three of our steers having had their brands changed? You knew that yesterday. Them wranglers only confirmed it.'

Dix swallowed and smiled broadly.

'Them brand-burners changed the marks on our steers.'

'We know that. So what?'

'But they must have changed them to look similar to a registered brand, Danny boy. They don't just burn other folks' brands off the hides of the rustled steers, they have to make them look like another *real* brand. Right? That's how they can sell them.'

Shaw placed his spoon in the bowl and chewed the pie in his mouth thoughtfully.

'Heck! I never thought of that,' he admitted.

'That's why this bunch of brand-burners have been so successful. They are experts at making nearly every brand seem the same as the one they've registered themselves. That takes a lot of skill.'

'But we still ain't no closer to catching them darn rustlers.'

Tom Dix scooped up his eggs and placed them all in his eager mouth. The satisfied expression made his partner laugh.

'It ain't the rustlers we have to catch. It's whoever owns that brand,' Dix said after he swallowed.

'Which brand?'

Tom Dix waved at the waitress and pointed at the bowl of apple-pie. He then looked straight back at his confused pal.

'The one on the three steers they rebranded, Dan. All we gotta do is make a copy of it and go find out who registered it at the Cattlemen's Association.'

Dan Shaw looked up at the ceiling.

'Of course! It's obvious, ain't it?'

'I knew you'd say that.' Dix nodded. He pushed his plate into the centre of the table and finished his coffee. 'How come I thought of it and you didn't?'

Dan Shaw began eating his pie again.

'OK. You figured it out and I didn't have a clue, Dixie. Reckon I ain't got such a devious mind as you. Maybe my honesty holds me back a tad.'

The waitress returned with a bowl of pie and placed it next to Dix's left hand.

'Tell me, Susan. Do you like older men?' Dix asked with a wry smile on his face.

She pouted for a moment.

'I reckon so. I like my pa. He's old like you two.'

'That makes him real old, Susan.' Dix nodded.

'Ancient,' Dan added.

'That's the word. Ancient.' The waitress beamed as only females of a certain youthful age could. She bounced away from their table happily.

Dix glanced at Dan and raised his eyebrow again. They both laughed out loud.

The massive George Washington steam locomotive had made good time since leaving Julesberg in Colorado with its three passenger-cars and solitary freight-car. It had managed to maintain over twenty miles an hour for the entire journey and had exceeded that speed more than once on the steep inclines along the way.

The gradient on the approach to Cheyenne was another place where the magnificent engine came into its own. A full head of steam had seen it cut a full thirty minutes off its scheduled timetable.

The engineer had been hanging on the whistle rope to alert the occupants of the bustling cattle town of their early arrival as he eventually allowed the train to slow.

Only the deaf and the dead were oblivious to the fact that the George Washington had entered Cheyenne and was moving through the array of cattle pens which lined both sides of the four sets of glistening steel tracks.

Steam gushed from both sides of the train as it ground to a halt next to the telegraph office, placed amid the pens which lined the rails.

No sooner had the train stopped than its attendants jumped down from the trio of passenger cars with their wooden steps in hand. The neatly uniformed men carefully placed the steps on the ground so that their valued customers would not have to leap the last three feet from the carriages' metal observation platforms on to the dusty ground. They then took up positions next to the steps to expertly assist the disembarking passengers and accept any tips they might be given.

Sheriff Harper rubbed his eyes for the umpteenth time as he stood beside his deputy watching the carriages and the passengers within their plush interiors, who started to rise from the luxurious padded leather seats and gather their belongings together before disembarking.

'Who we meeting, Rufas?' Seth Green asked, leaning on a worm-eaten upright outside the telegraph office.

Harper turned, then dragged the dishevelled figure upright and brushed him down with his gloved hands.

'How do I know? But when ya gets a wire telling you to meet a bigwig off the train, that's what ya do. You go and meet them, whoever they are.'

'What's a bigwig anyways?'

'Somebody rich or important, I guess.'

'Who sent that wire, Rufas?' Green asked, rubbing his nose along his sleeve. 'Coz whoever it was, they sure seem to have put a fox in your henhouse.'

Harper straightened his clothing and rubbed his eyes again and tried to make out the figures who were making their way down the steps which had been provided by the train's dutiful attendants.

'I ain't sure who sent it. But I got me some important friends and one of them must have thought that I needed warning about this *hombre.* He must be mighty important.'

'Are you scared?'

Harper's eyes narrowed.

'You and me both know that this is the sweetest

job we ever had. I ain't hankering to lose it. This so-called bigwig might be a powerful varmint from back East. Maybe one of them railroad bosses who can order the mayor or Cheyenne town council to fire us or he'll move his railtracks someplace else. Yeah, I'm scared, Seth.'

Green pulled out his tobacco-pouch and slid a paper between his brown-stained fingers.

'Want a smoke, Rufas? Ya look kinda edgy.'

Harper stamped his boot on the ground.

'Put that tobacco away, Seth. Ain't you been listening to me at all?'

'Why should I? It's more likely that it's some banker who wants to build a bigger bank than the ones we already got. Don't fret so much.'

'You could be right but I doubt it.' Harper polished his sheriff's star with the cuff of his shirt-sleeve and then squinted at the large square windows of the passenger cars. The sun was reflecting off the polished glass, making it almost impossible to make out anything with any certainty. 'Keep your eyes peeled for somebody who looks important.'

'Who's that?' Green asked, turning his head and nodding in the direction of a stout man in well-tailored eastern-designed clothing. 'He's even got a top hat. Is that him?'

There was a slight hint of panic in the sheriff's face and voice as he gritted his teeth and tried to work out how he would recognize someone he did not even know the name of.

'He does look important, don't he?'

'Yep. He sure does. But so does that critter down near the freight-car.' Green ran his tongue along the gummed edge of the cigarette paper before twisting it expertly between his thumb and index finger.

'Who?' Harper's head darted back and forth to each of the temporary sets of wooden steps that dozens of passengers were using to come down from the train's high cars. 'Who exactly is you lookin' at, Seth?'

'Him,' Green replied. He tucked the cigarette in the corner of his mouth and nodded to his left. 'That tall *hombre* in the long frock-coat. The dude with the long hair.'

Rufas Harper took a step forward to try and see over the heads of the passengers who were filtering into Cheyenne. He stretched to his full height, then rose up on to his toes.

Then he saw him.

Harper lowered himself back down and exhaled heavily as he glanced at the face of his bored deputy.

'I reckon that's him.'

Green narrowed his eyes, lit his cigarette and blew out the match with smoke.

'Are you OK, Rufas? You've gone a real unhealthy shade of white.'

'You'd be this colour if'n you knew who that was.'

'As far as I can tell he's just a real strange-looking dude, Rufas.' Green inhaled deeply and then allowed the smoke to drift through his flared nostrils.

'Don't let his looks fool ya, boy. I know that varmint.' The sheriff was now sweating from every part of his body. It had nothing to do with the noon temperature. It was the sweat of a man who was scared.

'Who in tarnation is he?'

'C'mon.' Harper grabbed Green's sleeve and walked towards the figure who was standing on the passenger-car steps studying his surroundings carefully.

Few if any men had ever cut such an imposing image in the eyes of the Cheyenne residents who looked in his direction. He was tall, lean and dressed like a riverboat gambler. His eyes were hooded, giving the false impression that he was half-asleep when in reality he was wide awake. A brown moustache covered his mouth. His hair was unusually long and hung over his wide shoulders from beneath a black flat-crowned John B. Stetson hat. It was if he was from another time. A time when mountain men trail-blazed the wilderness, long before barbers arrived with their scissors and straight razors.

Yet he was a rare type who had become a living legend for his courage and stylish eccentricity. His fame had spread across the entire continent through the countless dime novels which had been written about him. He was a man who defied anyone to better him with either guns or a deck of cards.

He was dangerous!

Two pearl-handled gun grips poked out from the unique hand-tooled gunbelt which had its holsters reversed. This was no ordinary visitor who had arrived in Cheyenne and the sheriff knew it.

This was the king of the cross-draw.

Both men walked through the disembarking passengers towards the imposing figure. When the man's head turned and looked down at them, they stopped.

Harper and Green were a matter of only thirty feet from the tall immaculately dressed man, yet the sheriff felt that they might regret their close proximity. The hooded eyes had frozen them to the spot when focused upon them.

'Who is he?' Green asked quietly out of the corner of his mouth after he had pulled the cigarette from his dry, cracked lips. 'He don't look nothing but a fancy dude to me. How come ya so troubled, Rufas?'

Sheriff Harper swallowed hard but there was no spittle in his mouth. He cleared his throat and tried vainly to mop the sweat off his rugged features with the tails of his bandanna.

'Don't ya recognize him, Seth? Ain't ya seen the pictures on them books in the hardware store?'

Green tilted his head and sucked on his cigarette again until he could feel the heat burning his fingers. He dropped what was left of it on to the dusty ground and stepped on it.

'Now ya mention it, he does look kinda familiar. But I'm damned if I knows where I've set eyes on him before. Is he a gambler?'

Harper nodded slowly. He tried to take his own eyes away from the piecing stare of the man who was watching them like a hawk watches its chosen prey before swooping out of the sky and striking.

'He's a gambler and a few other things, Seth. That's one varmint I never wanted to meet again.'

'Other things?' Seth Green pushed his hat-brim off his face and tried to work out where he had seen the familiar image before. 'What sort of other things?'

'A war hero. A gunfighter, a marshal and a lot of other things. If he's in Cheyenne, there has to be a reason. The critter who sent me the wire must have thought so anyway. I don't like it, Seth.'

'I still can't recall where I've seen him before.' Green bit his lower lip. 'What's his name?'

Sheriff Harper was about to reply when the man's low powerful voice drifted over them.

'If it ain't Rufas Harper. I ain't seen you in a coon's age, you lowlife river scum. Who made you a sheriff?' The man tossed a coin into the hands of the attendant below him and nodded at the broad smile.

'Thank you kindly, sir.' The attendant touched the black shining peak of his cap and then ran down towards his fellow workers.

'Don't the folks around here know about your colourful past, Rufas?' the man called out again from his high vantage point atop the wooden steps. 'Or is everyone in this stinking town as corrupt as you?'

Seth Green's mouth fell open. He turned his head and stared at the sheriff's face. Sweat dripped from Harper's jaw like rain.

'You gonna let him talk to ya like that, Rufas?' Seth Green asked.

Harper's eyes darted to his deputy before returning to the imposing figure of the man. He could not disguise the fear which had consumed his entire being.

'Yep. I'm letting that man say anything he damn well likes, Seth.'

'Why?'

'Coz only a man who's real tired of living argues with the likes of Wild Bill Hickok.'

EIGHT

Seth Green's face altered dramatically when he absorbed the name that had fallen from his friend's lips. He stared with more intensity at the tall lean figure standing on the top of the wooden steps. The name of Wild Bill Hickok had taken on an almost mythical quality on account of all the stories which had been written about him over the previous dozen or so years. The fictional dime novels and the reality were so closely entwined that even the man himself found it hard to know which was which.

Hickok had become a war hero long ago. From there his flamboyant nature had ensured that his fame grew with every heartbeat.

Yet Seth Green found it difficult to accept that the man with the long flowing hair could be anything like his reputation would suggest.

Like so many others before him, he was judging

the book by its cover, making the mistake which so many had done in the past.

'He don't look so tough to me, Rufas.' Green spat. 'I reckon all them stories about him was made up by folks back East.'

'Hush up, Seth,' Harper urged. 'I know him. You don't. He could kill you before ya seen his gun leave its holster.'

Green shook his head.

'The varmint got his holsters on backwards, Rufas. How could he draw them hoglegs out and shoot them? He'd have to have his hands on the wrong way around.'

'Hush up, you dang fool.' Sheriff Harper walked closer to the man he had last met three years earlier. A man he feared more than any other.

'You want something?' Hickok asked drily.

'What are you doing here, Wild Bill?'

Hickok stepped down on to the dusty ground and looked straight through the sweating man.

'You didn't answer my question, Rufas.'

'What question?'

The long fingers of the renowned gunfighter touched the star on Harper's vest.

'Who made you sheriff?'

'I was elected fair and square by the citizens of Cheyenne, Bill.'

Hickok pulled a long cigar from his pocket, bit off its tip and placed it between his teeth.

'All I can say is, the folks of Cheyenne must be

darn bad at adding up, Rufas.'

'Let me light that for you.' Harper struck a match with his thumbnail and offered its flame to the tall man. Hickok bent down and sucked enough of the flame into his Havana to light it before blowing out the match.

'Much obliged.' Hickok nodded.

Rufas Harper mustered every ounce of his courage and took a step closer to the famed lawman. 'What are you doin' here, Bill? You on business or something?'

Hickok smiled wryly before turning away from the two nervous lawmen. He walked along to the freight-car and banged on the large wooden sliding door.

'Open up!' he demanded.

'What you got in there, Bill?' Harper asked coyly.

'Stop sweating, Rufas. I ain't gonna kill ya.' Hickok muttered before returning his attention to the carriage door.

'It just seems a tad strange that you've come to my town when nobody invited you.' The sheriff knew he was taking a risk by confronting Hickok.

Wild Bill Hickok turned his head and glared with his hooded eyes at both men. There was no sign or hint of any emotion on the chiselled face.

'How do you know whether I was invited or not, Rufas? Maybe the mayor figured Cheyenne needed a real lawman.'

'I thought you quit being a marshal, Bill.' Harper gulped.

'Maybe I did and maybe I didn't.'

Sheriff Harper attempted to swallow. His Adams's apple remained stuck in his throat as every ounce of saliva dried up inside his mouth.

'Open up in there,' Hickok shouted before banging the wooden door again with a clenched fist.

The large door eventually slid open.

'Sorry, Mr Hickok,' said a tiny man in black from inside the freight-car. 'I was taking me a nap. Have we arrived early?'

'Yep. The train made good time, Jonas,' Hickok replied.

Jonas Kirk had been a guard on the railroad for nearly twenty years and every one of those years had left its mark on the small nervous man.

'I'm so sorry. Please forgive me. I'll just get my ledger and make sure that I don't make any more mistakes,' Jonas said, walking around the interior of the freight-car tapping his pencil against his lips. 'Now where did I put that ledger?'

'That's OK, friend. All I want is my horse,' Hickok said. He watched a wooden ramp being brought from beside some of the cattle pens. Three railroad workers placed the top of the ramp against the side of the open freight car. The powerful arms of the labourers forced steel pins into the ramp's brackets until it was secured firmly.

'What sort of horse was it, Wild Bill?' Jonas Kirk asked over his horn-rimmed glasses. 'Can you describe it for me?'

'How many horses you got in there, Jonas?' Hickok sighed heavily.

'Just the one. Lovely chestnut stallion,' muttered the small man.

'That's my horse.' Hickok sighed again.

Jonas Kirk stopped.

'That's right. You're the only person on the train with a horse. Then it must be yours.'

Hickok blew out a line of smoke.

'I reckon you're right, Jonas. That must be my horse.'

The elderly man smiled.

'I knew we'd sort this out. Funny you getting all confused like that. Not remembering your own horse. You have to watch that kinda thing, Bill. It's a sign.'

'A sign of what, Jonas?'

'Old age.'

'What you doin' in Cheyenne, Bill?' Harper repeated his question. 'C'mon. Tell me the truth. What you sticking your nose into my town for?'

'Curiosity killed the cat,' Hickok quoted. 'Don't get too feline on me, Sheriff Harper.'

'You threatening me?' Harper asked.

'Maybe. Stop fretting. For all you know I'm in town to play me some poker. Or I might be hunting some bounty. You know me, Rufas. I'm flexible.'

Seth Green spat at the ground and moved defiantly towards Hickok.

'Ya know something, Hickok?'

'What, sonny?'

'I reckon that you is just an old dandy,' Green offered. 'How come they call ya Wild Bill? Ya don't look very wild to me. I seen women who look more dangerous than you.'

'Really?'

'Hush up, Seth,' Harper warned.

'I will not hush up, Rufas. This fancy critter arrives in Cheyenne and you go all scared. Look at him. He's a joke.'

Hickok pulled his frock-coat apart and showed the ivory grips of his guns to the snorting deputy.

'Got a silver dollar, sonny?'

'Nope. Why?' Green was about to step even closer when he saw the hands of the legendary figure moving faster than he could believe.

Suddenly the guns had been cross-drawn from their holsters and started to fire. Gunsmoke spewed from the barrels as the deafening noise echoed all around the railhead.

Green felt his hat being ripped from his head and then his holster severed from his gunbelt. Before he had time to blink, the guns had been returned to their holsters.

'W . . . what happened?'

'I might be wrong, but I'm sure I heard shots being fired, Wild Bill,' said Jonas as he held the reins of Hickok's prized horse and urged him towards the ramp.

'Reckon so, Jonas.' Hickok watched as his horse was led out of the freight car and down towards the ground. He removed the cigar from his lips and moved closer to Green.

'The name happens to be James Butler Hickok, sonny. But for some damn reason folks keep calling me Wild Bill. Can you figure out why?'

Seth Green felt a trickle of blood running through his smouldering hair and down his face.

'I think so, sir.'

Hickok tapped the ash from his cigar, then patted the deputy's cheek and glanced at the sheriff.

'Keep that nose clean, Rufas.'

Harper nodded silently. He watched Hickok accept the reins from Jonas Kirk and then mount the tall chestnut stallion in one graceful movement.

Wild Bill Hickok slipped his long fingers into his vest-pocket and pulled out a gleaming US marshal's badge. He pinned it to the lapel of his frock-coat and nodded.

'Does that answer any of your questions, Sheriff?'

Harper forced a smile.

'Reckon it does, Bill.'

The tall rider spurred his mount and rode between the cattle pens into the heart of the town.

'So his name ain't really Wild Bill then, Rufas?' Green muttered as his fingers wiped the blood off his face.

'Will you just hush up!' Harper shouted. 'Ya gonna get us both killed, you idiot.'

NINE

The town hall was three storeys tall, a red-brick building which looked strangely out of place amid the far smaller wooden structures along the main street. Only the banks that dominated the town square came anywhere close to the sheer size and opulence of the magnificent edifice.

Tom Dix nudged Dan Shaw's elbow as they stood on the bottom step and looked up.

'Reckon Cheyenne must be doing OK, Dan.'

Dan nodded and removed his Stetson as they began the climb up the ten concrete steps toward the huge solid oak doors.

'I think you're right, Dixie,' Dan agreed.

The interior of the building was far cooler than the street temperature. The marble floor and walls ensured that the men inside this place did not break out in a sweat during office hours.

'Have you ever seen such a place?'

'Nope.'

A tall man who looked more like an undertaker than anyone else they had ever seen approached them with his hands clasped as if in prayer. He had a face that looked as if he could smell something he did not like under his long pointed nose.

'Can I help you, gentlemen?'

'That depends,' Dix replied.

'Upon what?' The man's expression did not alter.

'Do you have records of cattle brands in here?' Dan Shaw chipped in.

The man moved his fingers.

'Of course.'

Dix stepped closer to the official-looking man.

'Could we see those records?'

'Why would you wish to do that?'

'We want to check out who owns this brand.' Dan Shaw held out a scrap of paper with a drawing on it. It was the brand to which the rustlers had altered theirs.

The man gave a fleeting glance at the strange mark that Dix had drawn on the paper down at the cattle pens. He then looked down his nose again at the pair of men before him.

'I don't understand.'

'Brand-burners rustled our herd and changed

our brands to look like this one,' Dix explained. 'We figured that whoever owns this registered mark is the *hombre* behind the rustling.'

The man seemed slightly concerned.

'Wait here.'

Tom Dix and Dan Shaw watched the man walk across the polished marble floor and into a room. The sound of the heavy door being close echoed off the walls around them.

'What you figure is going on, Dan?'

Shaw was thoughtful.

'I'm not sure.'

'That face of his looked like we hit a nerve,' Dix added.

'You took the words right out of my mouth.' Dan nodded. 'I got me a feeling that critter knows something about the rustling around here.'

Dix sighed heavy. 'You could be right, *amigo.*'

For what seemed like an eternity the two men waited as instructed. Then the strange man returned with an envelope clutched between his hands.

Dix accepted the outheld envelope from the man.

'What is this?'

'Your appointment to look at the records,' the man replied nervously.

'We want to check them now.' Dan pulled the envelope from his partner's hand and opened it. He shook the folded notepaper and read it.

'What's going on here?'

'I don't understand.' The man lied.

'What's wrong, Dan?'

'It says here that we can check the brand registration records on the first of next month, Dixie,' Dan muttered.

'That's three weeks from now.'

The man went to turn but Tom Dix's hand grabbed his forearm in a firm grip and held him in check.

'Explain this, mister.'

What little colour there was in the man's face seemed to disappear as his small eyes looked at the veteran gunfighter. He swallowed.

'You have to have an appointment, sir.'

'But three weeks?' Dix queried. 'We can't afford to hang around Cheyenne for three weeks, mister. We got stock to drive back to our ranch.'

'Rules are rules, sir,' the man managed to say.

Dan Shaw shook his head at his partner. Dix released his grip and watched the man hurry away from them.

'We have to check those brand registrations, Dan.'

Dan Shaw inhaled deeply and led his friend back into the blazing sunshine. The two men replaced their hats and pulled down the brims to protect their eyes.

'We will, Dixie,' Dan muttered angrily.

TEN

James Butler Hickok eased back on his black reins and studied the exterior of the Little Dice. He had seen so many similar-looking saloons in his years wandering the length and breadth of the Wild West, that they had all become identical in his memory. There was an aroma which identified saloons to the knowledgeable. It was the mixture of stale beer, cigar smoke and gamblers' sweat. Of all the saloons Hickok had ridden past, this one was the most fragrant.

There was one difference with this town though. The streets of Cheyenne were far wider than in most towns yet they were filled with all sorts of vehicles, riders and people going about their habitual daily routines.

The famous lawman had felt the curious eyes watching his every move since he had ridden away from the railhead and through the maze of streets. No one had ever seen anything remotely like the striking appearance of Hickok before.

Then he heard the muffled recognition.

'Is that Wild Bill Hickok?'

'It has to be.'

'I never imagined he was so tall.'

'Look at his hair.'

'Look at the eyes.'

'Look at those guns.'

'What's Wild Bill doin' in Cheyenne?'

'He's wearing a marshal's badge.'

'This must be serious.'

'Somebody's going to die.'

Wild Bill dismounted from the high-shouldered chestnut stallion and looped his reins carefully over the hitching pole. He secured them with a tight knot and then stepped up on to the boardwalk and surveyed the street from one end to the other.

Men and women gave the tall stranger with hair that reached half-way down his back a wide berth. The stern, unchanging expression upon his face had a haunting appearance which deterred folks from being too curious.

Most realized who he was from seeing his likeness on countless dime-novel covers, whilst others only saw the carefully groomed image, an image which Hickok had honed over decades until he had reached almost mythic status.

His legend preceded him.

Hickok liked it that way.

Then there were the few who neither recognized him or even knew of his well-documented exploits.

These people were usually ignorant trail-hands who had no idea of what danger lay within the heart of the quiet, handsome man. Most could neither read nor write and their only use for newspapers was to tear them into strips and hang on string in an outhouse. Ignorance, they say, is bliss. It could also be a fatal flaw.

But of all those who observed him, each one saw someone who was different. A man who did not conform to the unwritten rules by which most men mindlessly abided.

A man who dared to be an individual.

Hickok appeared to be from another age. An age when men grew their hair long and hunted the once-abundant buffalo. Like the buffalo, his kind were now almost extinct.

But simply being different was in itself dangerous, for it drew the foolish like flies to a horse's tail.

Yet Wild Bill Hickok was used to every differing reaction his unusual appearance provoked in those who cast their eyes in his direction.

He could almost close his eyes and sense when trouble came anywhere close to him and his prized pearl-handled Colts. A thousand other saloons had trained him to know who would try their luck.

So it was as he stared along the boardwalk at the group of three cowboys heading noisily towards him. It was obvious that they had been paid off after bringing in a herd of cattle to Cheyenne and, like so many cowboys before them, had managed to drink most of their hard-earned wages in the numerous drinking dens within the boundaries of the large township.

At first Hickok heard only the familiar laughter and raised voices. Then he focused hard on them and watched the pointing fingers. When the rest of the street fell quiet, as if knowing what was likely to happen, Wild Bill could hear the insults clearly.

Hickok turned and rested his knuckles on his hips.

He had heard the same stupidity spewing from the lips of similar fools so many times. It was always exactly the same insults. And the laughter was the same too. For cowboys were not the best-informed of people and most of them had little if any education.

Hickok continued to stare at the trio of cowboys in their filthy trail-gear as they drew closer and closer to the object of their ridicule.

'Look yonder, boys! What have we here?' one of the cowboys screamed out. 'Let's go get us some fun with that critter.'

Wild Bill sighed heavily before flicking the safety loops off his gun hammers. Once again he was going to have to prove himself to a few unworthy fools, he thought.

Then his eyes noted the sheriff and his deputy guiding their mounts toward the Little Dice saloon. This was no coincidence and Wild Bill knew it. Hickok had expected them to follow and they had done so. They had trailed him from the railtracks as if frightened of what he might find in Cheyenne. They wanted to keep a close eye on the US marshal and were incapable of disguising the fact from his knowing eyes.

But Hickok could not be bothered with Harper or Green. The words which were being aimed at him from the three cowboys drew his attention back to them.

The insults kept coming.

'Look at that girl with the moustache, boys.'

'Don't she look purty?'

'What ya reckon it is? A man or a woman?'

'Wanna kiss a cowboy, dear?'

'Reckon she likes men the way we likes girls!'

As he stepped forward towards the approaching cowboys Hickok could see, out of the corner of his right eye, the sheriff and his deputy dismounting.

Other men and women quickly crossed the street between the tall marshal and the three ranting cowboys. Soon only Hickok and the trio of trail drivers were on the boardwalk outside the Little Dice. Those who had fled all stood across the street, watching and waiting for something to happen.

For it was obvious that something *was* going to happen.

Even the undertaker stepped out from his

impressive funeral parlour with his tape-measure hanging around his neck as if waiting to claim the bodies.

Hickok continued walking until he was a mere ten feet away from the three drunken cowboys. They all stopped and seemed to use each other as crutches as the effects of the hard liquor began to weaken their legs, but not their spirit or stupidity.

'You talkin' to me, children?' Hickok muttered in a low deliberate tone that caused their eyes to find his emotionless features. 'I don't care for being insulted by foul-smelling saddlebums.'

The cowboys swayed in unison and waved their hands at him.

'You sound like a man,' one of them said with a laugh.

'But ya still look like a girl.'

'A girl with a moustache.'

Wild Bill lowered his head until his chin touched his silk cravat. His eyes seemed to widen as the controlled fury welled up inside him.

'Ever seen a dead cowboy?' Hickok asked.

The cowboy in the centre of the trio swaggered forward and rested his hand on the grip of his gun.

'You threatenin' us, missy?'

'Yep,' Hickok answered.

The two other cowboys started to toy with their own guns.

'Get out of our way, dude,' one of them growled.

'Yeah. We'll kill ya damn quick if'n ya don't.'

Hickok nodded.

'Reckon I owe you a warning. They call me Wild Bill Hickok and that might make you boys want to reconsider using them hoglegs.'

'We ain't scared.'

'I never heard of ya!'

'Wild Bill ain't a real person,' the third cowboy piped up defiantly. 'He's just in them story-books. Get out of our way, missy.'

Hickok exhaled heavily.

'You gonna apologize, children?'

'Nope,' snarled the closest cowboy.

'Then you'll regret ever meeting me,' Wild Bill said grimly.

'Get him, boys!' the second cowboy shouted suddenly.

At once the three cowboys' drunken hands fumbled for their weaponry. The guns were somehow drawn from their crude holsters. One fell from the fingers of the closest cowboy whilst his two companions managed to raise and aim theirs at the tall figure before them.

The choking gunsmoke blackened the distance between them as the deafening sound echoed off all the buildings in the street.

As Hickok felt the bullets pass him, he drew one of his weapons and fanned its hammer three times in quick succession.

He placed a well-aimed bullet into each of the cowboys and watched them flying into the dusty street. Then Wild Bill stared down at the wounded men and blew the smoke from the barrel of his Colt.

'You're lucky I'm not in a killing mood, children,' he said.

Harper and Green came rushing towards him shouting at the tops of their voices.

'Ya can't go round my town shooting folks!' the sheriff shouted at the tall US marshal.

'He's loco, Rufas,' Green added.

Hickok pulled the spent shells from his gun and tossed them aside. His long fingers slid fresh bullets into the hot chambers.

'They ain't dead.' Hickok sighed.

'I ought to arrest you, Bill!' Rufas Harper waved a finger at the taller man. 'Arrest you, lock you up and throw away the damn key!'

Hickok looked down into the sheriff's eyes and smiled.

'Don't ever try, Rufas. I'd hate to waste a bullet on your miserable hide.'

One of the cowboys managed to struggle back on to his feet. Blood was flowing freely from a hole in his shoulder.

'You bastard!' the cowboy screamed, raising his gun again. 'I'm gonna kill ya this time.'

Harper ducked and waved his hands at the wounded man.

'Don't be a fool.'

The cowboy squeezed the trigger. A plume of

deadly venom exploded from the gun barrel.

Wild Bill felt the heat of the bullet as it passed within inches of his face. He raised his own gun and fanned its hammer once then turned and walked towards the saloon swing-doors.

A neat bullet hole went between the eyes of the cowboy. The back of the man's head shattered in a mangled mess of red gore before the body slumped lifelessly on top of his two groaning companions.

'Hickok!' yelled Sheriff Harper.

James Butler Hickok paused for a brief moment with his left hand on top of the swing-doors.

'I really hate cowboys!' Hickok muttered. 'There ain't a brain between the whole bunch of them.'

Before Harper could say another word, the tall man had entered the saloon, leaving the doors swinging back and forth in his wake.

ELEVEN

Tom Dix and Dan Shaw had walked the better part of a quarter-mile from the town hall in the direction of the Cheyenne Hotel, when they both stopped at exactly the same time and raised their favoured gun hands to point at the familiar saddle.

There was no mistaking the hand-tooled black saddle with its silver decoration and matching bridle. It was yet another piece in the jigsaw which had helped make James Butler Hickok a legend in his own lifetime.

No ordinary saddle would be good enough for Wild Bill.

'Do you see what I see, partner?' Dan asked in total disbelief.

'It can't be,' Dix answered. 'Can it?'

'That's what I was going to say, Dixie.'

'But it sure looks like his saddle.'

Dan rubbed his wrinkled eyes and focused.

'What would he be doing here?'

Tom Dix pointed to the long sign above the building in front of which the solitary horse was tied up. THE LITTLE DICE SALOON was painted big and bold.

'I might be wrong but ain't that a saloon, Dan?'

'That it is. The Little Dice saloon according to the fancy sign,' Dan answered.

'And they got whiskey and gambling in saloons. Two of Bill's favourite things, as I recall.' Dix smiled.

Dan Shaw shrugged. 'You forgot the other thing that he's partial to, Dixie. They got that in there as well.'

'That's a darn tall horse,' Dix noted knowingly.

'The sort that he favours.'

'That horse has vinegar by the looks of it.'

'A lot of vinegar, I'd say,' Dan agreed.

Both men stepped up on to the raised boardwalk and made their way slowly along towards the saloon's swing-doors. The closer they got to the magnificent chestnut stallion the more they knew that this horse had to belong to their long-time friend, the unique James Butler Hickok.

Dan Shaw studied the bridle carefully.

The silver initials JBH were set into the black leather livery. He had seen it many times before.

'This is Bill's horse OK,' Dan said. He straightened up and turned to his friend, who was looking over the swing-doors into the smoke filled interior of the Little Dice. 'Unless someone bushwhacked him and stole it.'

Dix laughed.

'There ain't no such animal capable of getting the drop on old Wild Bill, Dan.'

'How can you be so sure, Dixie?'

'Coz I'm looking straight at the old varmint playing cards, *amigo.*'

Shaw moved closer to his friend.

'With his back to the wall?'

'Yep.' Dix looked over his partner's shoulder. His eyes screwed up as he focused. He pointed at the dried red blood which was splattered over the ground next to the boardwalk. 'Looks like there's been some gunplay recently, Dan.'

Dan Shaw strode to the nearest wooden upright and ran a gloved hand over a fresh bullet hole. The splinters fell away and landed on to the sun-bleached boards. He looked at the dried blood and then returned silently to Tom Dix's side.

'How much do ya want to bet that Wild Bill had something to do with that, Dixie?'

'Only a fool bets against a certainty, Dan. C'mon.' Dix pushed the swing-doors inward and entered the busy saloon. Dan followed a mere step behind the aged gunfighter. They made their way across the sawdust floor and navigated between the numerous round tables until they reached the one where a very serious game of poker was in full flow.

Dix and Dan stopped a few feet from the table.

They looked down at the four other players who had chosen to take on one of the West's best card-players. It was hard to tell whether Hickok had noticed them or not as he had the brim of his Stetson pulled down over his brow.

Only the four other card-players could see the eyes of the legendary figure, who chewed on a long, slim, unlit cigar. But Wild Bill Hickok was the king of the poker-faces as well as the cross-draw. His classic features gave nothing away.

Dix looked at Dan and then cast his eyes on the pile of coloured chips in the centre of the table. There were only a few chips left in front of the five men.

The stakes were high.

They always were when Hickok played poker.

'You ready to fold, Hickok?' one man asked.

'Don't rush me, sir. I'm weighing up the odds,' Wild Bill responded as he thoughtfully shuffled his five cards in his long slender fingers. 'It seems to me that we've darn near exhausted our funds.'

'OK,' another man muttered as he counted and recounted what few chips he had left. 'What ya getting at, Hickok?'

'I calculate that there is only two hundred dollars in front of all of us,' Hickok observed. 'Hardly enough to make this game reach its true potential.'

'So what?' snapped the man closest to Hickok's right.

'You gonna raise the bet, Bill? asked the man to Hickok's left. 'If'n you are, you'll need more chips.'

Hickok said nothing as he kept shuffling his cards.

'It's your play, Bill.'

Dix and Shaw kept watching in silence. They knew that this game was at a crucial stage and only a fool interrupted poker-players when they had most of their chips sitting in the pot.

'For God's sake play, will ya?' begged the man directly opposite Wild Bill. 'I've got to get back to my office.'

At last Hickok placed his cards face down before him and looked around at the four other men.

His hooded eyes gave nothing away.

'How much do you figure is in the pot, boys?'

The men muttered amongst themselves before reaching a rough estimate.

'Must be two thousand dollars there, Bill,' one of them said. 'Why?'

Hickok nodded in agreement.

'That's what I figured.'

There was a long silence until the player to Hickok's right cleared his throat.

'What you thinkin'?'

Hickok put the long fingers of his right hand inside his frock-coat, pulled out a long leather wallet, then dropped it on top of the chips.

'That's exactly what I've got in my wallet, boys.

Hundred-dollar bills. Twenty of the critters.'

One of the men went to touch the wallet when Hickok raised his voice.

'Don't you trust Wild Bill Hickok, sir?'

The hand stopped and was quickly withdrawn.

'Sure we trust you, Bill. But we don't understand.'

'I've covered every cent in the pot.' Hickok sighed. 'Are you boys brave enough to gamble?'

'You mean show our cards?' asked the player to his left.

'Nope. You toss all your cards into the pot and then we each take one from the deck in turn. Highest card wins everything.'

There were simultaneous gasps from the four players, who had never heard of such a thing. They began to argue. Some knew that they had good hands and others bad. The men with the poor hands were praying that they could bluff their way to winning the pot.

'I'm playing poker, Hickok!' the man at Hickok's right snorted. 'We play our cards.'

'I don't like it, Bill. I have a darn good hand,' said another.

'But that sure is a juicy pot and no mistake.' The player across the table shrugged. 'I reckon Wild Bill has come up with a mighty interesting idea, boys.'

The player on Hickok's left looked even more troubled. 'All of it for the highest cut of what's left of the deck? That ain't poker. That's loco. I'm against it, dammit.'

'I don't like it either,' another agreed.

Hickok pushed himself back in his chair until its front legs lifted off the ground and wooden back touched the wall behind him He rested one of his boots on the edge of the green baize and struck a match. He sucked in the smoke and then stared through it at his nervous opponents.

'You boys scared? I thought you were gamblers.'

The men suddenly went quiet.

'Most of the good cards have already been dealt. What's left in the deck is questionable. I'm willing to risk it. Are you?'

'There are rules in poker, Bill.'

Hickok pulled the cigar from his lips and placed it in a glass ashtray. He lowered himself back until the chair's front legs were on the ground again.

'OK. Then match my two thousand.'

The men looked at what was left of their chips.

'We ain't got that much left.'

'I'll accept whatever you got. Throw them chips in and let's turn over our cards.'

Reluctantly the men threw in the last of their coloured gaming chips and looked at the long-haired man with a marshal's badge to his lapel.

Wild Bill Hickok pointed his cigar at the man to his left.

'What you got?'

The player inhaled deeply and then turned over

his cards. A sigh of relief went around the other players with the exception of Hickok, who remained unmoved.

'Queen high? That was sure an optimistic game you played, mister,' observed Hickok.

The next poker-player spread his cards out on the green baize.

'Two pair. Fives and eights,' Hickok said aloud. 'Not a bad hand.'

The third man placed his five cards down.

'Another two pairs. Tens and nines. A tad better.' Hickok turned to the last player and glared at him. His hooded eyes seemed to burn into the player. 'Your turn.'

The last player seemed to think that he had the beating of Hickok. He smiled and slowly placed each card down, one at a time.

All eyes were on the cards.

A ten. Then four kings.

'Can you beat that, Bill?' the player asked as if he somehow already knew the answer. 'Show them five cards of yours and lets see just how good the famous Wild Bill Hickok is.'

There was no movement in Hickok's features.

He picked up his cards and looked at them with unblinking eyes, then stared at the face of the smiling card-player.

'Yep. I can beat that hand,' he said calmly.

The player's face could not disguise his bewilderment at the words which came from the mouth behind the drooping brown moustache.

'You can?' The player gasped.

'Yep!' Hickok dropped his cards on to the table face up, but did not take his eyes from the player next to him.

'Four aces?' The man growned angrily. 'That can't be.'

Hickok continued to stare at the man.

'Why not?'

'You must have cheated, Bill,' snarled the man. He banged his clenched fists on the table. 'There's no way you could have four aces.'

Hickok kept looking at the irate player. There was no hint of any emotion behind the hooded stare.

'How could you possibly know that I did not have four aces, mister? Maybe because you dealt out the hands? Ain't these the ones you gave me from the bottom of the deck?'

The man pushed his chair away from the table and rose to his feet. His right hand moved under the flap of his coat. Hickok sat watching the gambler as the three other players hurriedly dived to the floor and crawled for cover.

The sound of terrified men and women filled the Lucky Dice saloon as everyone scrambled away from the card-table. Only two men remained firmly planted to the spot.

Tom Dix and Dan Shaw looked on helplessly.

They could do nothing except watch in horror

as the poker player pulled out a deadly .38 Smith & Wesson from its hidden shoulder holster.

Wild Bill continued to just sit and watch as the angry poker-player raised the gun and aimed it straight at him. Even then, the expression on Hickok's face remained the same. It was as if it were carved in stone.

'Ya gonna die, Hickok!' screamed the poker player.

Hickok did nothing until he saw the man's thumb touch the hammer of the gun and haul it back.

Only then did he react.

Both of Hickok's hands moved with a speed which defied anyone to focus upon them. His right hand pulled the gun from the left holster and the left hand drew the gun from the right one.

There was no man alive who could rival the speed of Hickok's cross-draw.

Both barrels blasted their deadly venom. The sound was deafening and continued to bounce off the saloon walls long after the bullets had found their target.

The card-player was lifted off the sawdust-covered floorboards and thrust backwards. With blood hanging on the gunsmoke-filled air, the lifeless gambler crashed on top of another card-table behind him.

Crimson streams ran freely out of the two neat

bullet holes in the middle of the card-player's chest. The half-cocked .38 fell from his fingers.

Silently, Hickok rose to his feet and holstered his smoking weapons. He removed his hat and shook his long hair free. The other poker-players continued to crawl through the sawdust towards the saloon's swing-doors.

As the acrid gunsmoke cleared, Tom Dix and Dan Shaw stepped closer to the card-table. They watched as Hickok scooped all the chips into the bowl of his hat and then picked up his wallet.

'If it ain't Tom Dix and Dan Shaw,' Wild Bill Hickok acknowledged. 'I thought I could smell something sweet.'

Dan touched his hat-brim. 'Good to see you, Bill. I see that things are pretty much the same for you.'

'Howdy, Dan.' Hickok glanced at the body of the dead gambler for a fleeting moment. He had lost count how many times he had had to prove himself with his trusty pair of pistols. It gave him no satisfaction to add another notch to his tally. 'That's the second dumb idiot I've had to kill since I arrived on the noon train. I reckon there must be a breed of people who just ain't cut out to live with other folks. They try and cheat their way to claiming the pot. Then there's the type who just trails the winner and sticks a knife or bullet in his back. There used to be a time when you could trust folks, boys.'

'Trouble ain't never been too far away,' Dan said.

'And it keeps doggin' my trail.' Hickok sighed. 'You'd think someone famous like me would never have anyone pull a gun on him, wouldn't you?'

'A lot of folks ain't read them dime novels, Bill.' Dan smiled.

'You're looking mighty good, James Butler Hickok,' said Dix, nodding. 'I swear that you never seem to change.'

'And you just get older every time we meet, Dixie.' Hickok grinned. 'How come? Don't you drink whiskey or something that will pickle your innards? A man needs a little help if'n he's gonna last long enough to lose all his teeth.'

'When did you first spot me and Dan, Bill?' Tom Dix was curious.

'Soon as you poked your ugly heads over the swing-doors, Dix. My eyes have been pretty good of late.'

'I'm a mite curious.' Dix rubbed his chin. 'How did you get those four aces, Bill?'

'Same way that he got the four Kings, Dixie.' Hickok slid his wallet back into his inside pocket and pointed at the gambler spread across the table. The famed gunfighter shook his head once more. 'I knew he was cheatin'. I had to do a little sleight of hand to make the varmint admit it.'

'And how much money is in your wallet, Bill?' Dan asked coyly. He'd known Hickok too long.

'There ain't nothing in my wallet until I cash these chips in, Daniel.' Wild Bill Hickok stood to his full impressive height and looked around the Little Dice again. Men and women seemed glued to the walls in their attempt to keep away from Hickok and his particular brand of justice.

'Still bluffing your way through the day.' Dix sighed. 'The same old James Butler.'

'Not bluffing, Dix,' Wild Bill corrected. 'Just making sure that things even out in the long run. I'll never cheat to win a few dollars, but if this poker-face of mine can scare someone who is considering the idea, so be it.'

Dan Shaw edged closer.

'I thought that you'd left it too late to draw them hoglegs, this time. I heard his gun cock before you even went for your weapons.'

'That particular model of Smith and Wesson has a strange mechanism, Dan.' Hickok told him. 'It has to be cocked back fully. It clicks three times before you can pull its trigger.'

'One day you'll leave it too late.'

'Wild Bill Hickok only draws in self-defence,' came the firm response.

'Why exactly are you in Cheyenne, Bill?' Dan asked, studying the coloured chips in the hat bowl. 'Not to play a few hands of poker. There has to be a better reason to bring you this far out of our way.'

Hickok nodded.

'You're right.'

'Then what would bring you here?'

James Butler Hickok sighed.

'Someone important figured I was needed in Cheyenne. Reckons the local law and politicians ain't been protecting the local cattle ranchers. They figured only Wild Bill could catch the varmints.'

Tom Dix smiled.

'So you're here to stop a bunch of brand-burners?'

Hickok picked up his cigar and blew the ash from its smouldering tip until it glowed again. He gripped it between his teeth and grunted.

'How does that matter to you, Dixie?'

'Coz that's why we're here, James Butler. We had our herd rustled. But we got them back. I almost rounded up the whole bunch of them but a lightning-bolt had other ideas.'

'The brand-burners are working for somebody, Dixie,' Hickok said firmly. 'Whoever it is, I'll get him.'

'We tried to check out the brand registrations at the town hall but they wouldn't let us,' Dan added.

Hickok nodded. 'That fits in with my information. I was told that whoever is pulling the strings, and making them rustlers dance, they must be darn important in Cheyenne.'

'If we could get a look at the brand registrations, we could see who owns the brand that them burners have been changing all the other ones to look like,' Dix told Hickok. 'The man who owns that brand is our man.'

'I thought we could break in to the town hall tonight and take us a look, Wild Bill.' Dan grinned.

'No need to break in, Danny boy.' Wild Bill winked. 'We find a judge and get us a warrant. They'll have to show us anything we want to look at if we have a warrant. That's the law.'

Hickok walked across the saloon with his gambling-chip-filled hat in his arms towards a pale cashier who stood behind a very inadequate desk and metal grille.

'A warrant, huh?' Dix was impressed. 'But I still think that the odds are stacked against any one man acting alone, James Butler. Can we tag along to help?'

'That's fine, boys. Real fine,' boomed Hickok. 'I'm in need of some reliable help if I'm to get to the bottom of this. And I can't think of two better men than you. You might be a tad old but I'll make you deputy marshals all the same. OK?'

'Yep,' said both men at once.

Rufas Harper pushed his way into the saloon with Green a few steps behind him. The sheriff sniffed the air and then spotted the dead gambler on top of the blood-soaked card-table. He ran up to Hickok and raged.

'Did you do that?'

'Sure did, Rufas.' Hickok smiled as he handed his hat of chips to the cashier. 'Self-defence. Ask anyone.'

Harper looked at Shaw and then Dix. Both men nodded in agreement with the US marshal.

'Self-defence, Sheriff,' Dix said.

'Tom Dix and his pal. I might have known it.' Harper snorted. Wild Bill rested an elbow on the cashier's desk and pulled the cigar from his lips.

'So you've met my deputies, have you, Rufas?'

'I don't believe this.' Harper turned and slapped Green across the shoulder. As they left the saloon they could hear the muffled laughter behind them.

TWELVE

It was a frustrated Mac Mason who opened the door of the large wooden cabin and strode to the edge of the steep cliff. He gazed down on the sprawling town of Cheyenne set in the fertile valley amid a million trees and green grass. For the first time since he had rounded up the eight other members of his gang, they had not managed to fulfil their orders. They had lost half their hand-made branding-irons and most of their guns in the unexpected turmoil which had almost cost them their liberty and lives. Only the intervention of God or, more than likely, Satan, had saved them from Tom Dix.

Mason was not a man who ran from danger but he had done just that the previous night. He had led his brand-burners out of the inferno and to their terrified horses. They had fled like scared rabbits to the safety of their hideout. He was angry. Angry that when faced with something he neither understood nor had anticipated, he had run away.

A hundred thoughts drifted through his mind at once.

Had he finally been shown to be nothing more than a craven coward? Was he actually no better than the men he surrounded himself with?

The thoughts soured his craw.

It left a bitter taste that no amount of spitting could get rid of. Mason had managed to replace the guns his men had left in the blazing building back in Cheyenne from the stockpile in their cabin, but the branding-irons were a different matter. They had been specially made.

Only a blacksmith could forge a new set for them.

All he had to do now was replace the hefty chunk of pride he had left behind him during the night. He had lost face and he knew it. Yet none of the men around him had shown themselves to be any braver. Mason nodded to himself as he stared down at the dry dusty ground. At least he had held on to his weapons even when Dix had ordered him to drop them.

Mason looked at the dust rising from the winding trail that led to his high vantage point. His keen hearing had detected the rider making his way up the steep hill long before any of his companions had.

He squinted hard and then nodded knowingly.

'Here comes Pete, boys.'

The rest of the brand-burners moved to the edge of the brittle cliff and stared down into the dust that rose from the hoofs of Pete Walker's struggling horse.

'Do you reckon he's got news from the boss, Mac?' Eli Payne asked Mason.

'You can ask him yourself when he gets here, Eli,' came the swift reply.

Toby Dwayne was, like half of the men around him, troubled. He had not liked facing the barrels of Tom Dix's pistols the previous night. For the first time since he had started riding with the infamous bunch of rustlers, he realized how close death was to their breed.

He and most of the brand-burners were thieves. None of them had ever been hardened killers apart from Mason. They could fire their weapons but they were not experts in the art of taking lives. The reality of being so close to death had not dawned on him, until now.

To steal cattle was a hanging offence in Wyoming as well as most other parts of the vast West. Only a rope would be required to administer their sentence.

Dwayne knew that if they were ever caught, there would be no trial with lawyers and a judge. For cattle-thieves were strung up high. High enough to warn others that cattlemen made their own laws. Toby Dwayne knew that most of his fellow rustlers felt the same and had only remained because they were even more afraid of Mason. None wanted to go against the wrath of their brutal leader.

Pete Walker reined in and dismounted hurriedly from his lathered-up mount. He rubbed the dust from his face and approached his fellow brand-burners.

'The boss is mighty angry about last night, Mac.'

Mason smacked a right fist into the palm of his left hand and growled like a hound-dog.

'The boss is angry, huh?'

'Yep. He sure is,' Walker said. Cal Smith handed him a canteen of cool clear water. He drank his fill and then rubbed his mouth on the back of his gloved left hand.

'The boss ain't got no damn right to be angry with us. Has he, boys?' Mason snarled. 'Was it our fault the storm scattered them steers?'

'You forget about Tom Dix, Mac?' Payne asked. 'He had a little to do with us losing them cattle.'

Mason stared at the seated figure with his cutting rope in his skilled hands. He spat across the distance between them.

'I'm startin' to think that you're a jinx, Eli. You just keep goin' on about Dix. Even if he'd not shown up we'd not have been able to brand them steers. The damn barn got hit by lightning and caught fire. Remember?'

'All I did was tell you that Dix wasn't the sort to quit trailin' folks. Not once he had their scent in his nostrils.' Payne said in a low tone. 'I know him. He'll not quit trackin' us. I bet he's still after us.'

'I still say you're a jinx.' Mason hit the air with his clenched fist. 'You're just bad luck, Eli. A whole bag of bad luck.'

Payne lowered his head and stared silently at the rope in his hands.

Jeb Olsen edged closer to Walker and rested a hand on the man's shoulder.

'What else did the boss say, Pete?'

'He's got another job for us,' Walker replied. 'But this ain't no rustlin' job. This time it's serious, Jeb.'

Mac Mason forced his way through the men gathered close to Walker and turned the younger man around forcefully.

'What kinda job are ya talkin' about, Pete? We can't go rustlin' any more herds until we replace our branding-irons.'

'Killing!' Walker sighed. 'The boss wants us to do some killing, Mac.'

The expression on Mason's face changed. Suddenly he looked as troubled as half his men.

'The boss wants us to do some killing?'

'Yep.'

Mason blinked hard. He looked at the ground and then back up into the features of Walker.

'Who does the boss want us to kill, Pete?'

'Tom Dix and his partner. A critter called Dan Shaw.'

Eli Payne got to his feet and carefully coiled his trusty rope. He shook his head and walked towards the group of muttering rustlers.

'Count me out, Mac. I'm ridin'.'

Mac Mason rubbed his whiskers and looked at the small man.

'Nobody quits, Eli! Not even a snot-nosed worm like you.'

Payne looped his rope over his shoulder and pushed the brim of his Stetson off his tanned brow.

'I ain't havin' no part of murder, Mac. I'm a wrangler who rustles steers, but I'm no killer. All I know how to do with any skill is to rope steers and bring the varmints down. What use am I to you if'n ya gonna murder Dix and Shaw?'

'Maybe that skill might be exactly what we need to bring Dix and his pal off their horses, Eli,' Mason said thoughtfully.

Payne exhaled heavily. 'I'm not havin' nothing to do with killing anyone, Mac.'

Mason grabbed Walker and pulled him close.

'Are you certain the boss wants us to kill Dix and his pal?'

'Yep.' Walker nodded. 'The boss says that they're gettin' too darn nosy about brands and such like. We have to kill the *hombres* or we'll all end up at the end of a noose.'

Mason released his grip on Walker. He then grabbed Payne's shirt and hauled him off his feet.

He stared straight into the older face and snorted like a raging bull.

'Hear that, Eli? We gotta do it. Or we'll all end up swinging from the end of a rope. I know you likes ropes but not enough to have ya neck snapped by one. Right?'

'Right,' Payne croaked fearfully.

The muscular Mason lowered Eli Payne until his high-heeled boots found the ground once more. Then he looked at the face of every man with the same brutal intensity that he had shown to Payne.

'I know that you boys ain't killers or even gunfighters for that matter, but it don't matter none. I've done me enough killin' for all of us. If the boss reckons we have to get rid of Dix and his pal, then that's what we do.'

'But how we gonna do it, Mac?' Sam Canute queried.

'There's only one way to get the better of a gunfighter like Tom Dix, Sam.' Mason snorted. 'We bushwhack the critter.'

The men began to think about it. They were indeed no match for the likes of Dix in a fair fight, and knew it. But to lure him into a trap made sense.

'I like that idea.' Canute grinned.

'Who do ya figure his partner is, Mac?' asked Dave Travis as he wondered how they were going to achieve this seemingly simple feat.

'Another gunfighter?' Olsen gulped.

'What if he is? A trap's a trap, boys.' Mac Mason laughed loudly. 'And the trapper always has the edge. We know where and when we are gonna ambush them. They don't. It don't matter none if Tom Dix is the best gunfighter in the West. He can't win this one.'

'When we doing this, Mac?' Smith ventured.

Mason looked at Walker.

'When does the boss want this done, Pete?'

'As soon as possible. The boss said there ain't no time to waste, Mac. We have to stop them before they find out the truth about the boss and us.'

'Saddle the horses, boys,' Mason ordered his men. 'We'll do it tonight. Tonight Tom Dix and his friend will die.'

Apart from the chuckling Mason, there was a grim silence amongst the other brand-burners.

THIRTEEN

It was late afternoon and the sun was low in the sky above Cheyenne. The sky was flaked with streaks of red as the three men dismounted and tied their horses to the hitching rail outside the handsome building. The impressive figure of Wild Bill Hickok led Dix and Shaw up the concrete steps and into the town hall. He did not stop and wait for anyone to confront him and then usher him back out into the wide street. The few men within the cool interior of the building shied away from the sight of the tall US marshal as his hooded eyes sought out and found his chosen goal. Hickok continued walking across the marble floor with Dix and Shaw in his wake until he reached an impressive door with a brass plate screwed to its centre which read JUSTICE D.L. COOPER.

'I reckon that this must be the place, boys.' Hickok turned the handle and walked into the outer office. A startled secretary stood, shaking, as the three men strode past her and into the judge's private office.

D.L.Cooper was a man who had an unruly mop of white hair and looked as if he would never see seventy again. He glanced up from his papers at the trio of men who had reached the opposite side of his large oak desk. There was no hint of surprise or trepidation in the elderly man.

'Can I help you, gentlemen?' Cooper asked.

'I want a warrant, Judge,' said Hickok, in a tone which seemed to rule out any form of refusal. 'I have to check the records of the Cattlemen's Association across the hall.'

The judge leaned back in his padded leather chair and tapped his lips with a pencil. His vivid blue eyes had seen many things in their time, but nothing to match the sight of Hickok in his hand-tailored trail gear. Wild Bill stood before the elderly judge in a fringed buckskin coat, white Stetson and black knee-high boots that almost covered his blue pants. Only the guns and their belt were the same as he had worn earlier.

'And you are. . . ?' D.L.Cooper asked curiously.

Wild Bill pulled his buckskin jacket apart to reveal the gleaming star.

'Hickok, sir. US marshal. These are my deputies.'

Cooper picked up a pipe and placed its stem between his gleaming store-bought teeth.

'The famed Wild Bill Hickok, I take it.'

'That's what they call me, sir.'

'Why do you wish to see the records of the Cattlemen's Association, Marshal.' The judge leaned forward, picked up a box of matches and shook it. He opened it and extracted a match.

'It's a long story, Judge Cooper,' replied Hickok.

'Do not allow my advanced years to worry you. I have plenty of time to listen, Marshal Hickok.' Cooper struck the match, put the flame above the pipe bowl and sucked its stem. 'Explain.'

Wild Bill sighed.

'I have been sent to Cheyenne to investigate why so many ranchers' cattle have been rustled.'

'I do not understand.' Cooper puffed.

'Someone in Cheyenne has hired a bunch who are experts at altering brands on cattle, sir,' Dix explained. 'These men have been using their skill to change existing brands to look like a real registered one.'

Judge Cooper removed his smoking pipe from his mouth and blew out the match.

'I begin to understand, Deputy.'

'These men are brand-burners,' Dan Shaw added.

'But they're working for someone else,' Hickok continued. 'We figure that the owner of the substituted brand is the man we're after.'

'Very interesting, Hickok.' Cooper nodded. 'Then I take it that the steers are sold as belonging to this certain character who owns the substituted brand?'

'Right!' Dan nodded.

'And then they are sold and shipped out of Cheyenne quite legally,' D.L. Cooper said aloud.

'I'm glad you understand, sir.' Hickok sighed. 'Can you please give us a search warrant?'

'Yes, Marshal Hickok. I shall be pleased to do so.' Cooper sat forward and struck a brass bell on his desk.

The nervous secretary entered the office cautiously.

'Yes, Judge Cooper?'

'Bring me a blank search-warrant, Kate,' Judge Cooper instructed.

'Yes, sir,' said the female. She returned to her own office.

Suddenly the sound of a raised voice echoed around the judge's chambers. It was the voice of Sheriff Harper as he too ignored the secretary and marched into the judge's private chambers.

'You in here, Wild Bill?'

Hickok turned and strode towards the open doorway and the sheriff, who had hesitated when seeing the gathered assembly.

'What do you want, Rufas?'

Sheriff Harper took one step into the office, then removed his hat when he saw the judge sitting at his desk with his pipe in his mouth. He touched his temple, then looked up into Hickok's features.

'I've been lookin' all over for you, Bill,' Harper whispered.

'What for?'

Harper unbuttoned his shirt and pulled out a folded scrap of paper. He handed it to the marshal.

'I got a note for your pal, Tom Dix, Bill. I figured that if I found you, I'd find him.'

'Why do ya want me, Sheriff?' Dix asked, curious.

Hickok shook the paper and began to read silently. When he had finished his eyes darted back at the sheriff.

'Is this on the level, Rufas?'

'Damned if I know, Bill.' Harper shrugged.

'Who gave you this?'

'It was poked under my office door when me and Seth returned earlier.' The sheriff was sweating. 'I've been looking for you for an hour or more.'

'Reckon someone plain like me is a tad hard to find, Rufas,' joshed the marshal.

Dix walked to Hickok's side and took the paper from his hands. He studied it carefully.

'Strange.'

'Sure is, Dixie,' agreed Hickok.

'What's wrong, gentlemen?' asked the judge through a cloud of pipe smoke. 'You seem somewhat alarmed. May I see that note, Mr Dix?'

Tom Dix turned away from the sheriff and

returned to the desk. He handed the note to the elderly judge.

'What is it, Dixie?' Dan asked.

'A note from the mayor of this town asking me and you to meet him a little while after sundown at a place called Painted Rock, Dan,' replied Tom Dix.

Judge Cooper looked up at Dix.

'I take it you have no idea what this is about?'

'None, sir.'

'I smell a trap, Mr Dix. It seems that someone wants to lure you and your pal out of town,' suggested Cooper.

Wild Bill stepped beside Dix and placed a hand on his lean shoulder. He looked down at the judge.

'This is my friend. And a finer man you could not wish to meet, Judge. Dixie here has saved my bacon a couple of times in the past, although I have repaid that debt in a more than generous way. But why would you say it was a trap?'

Cooper raised his white eyebrows and tried not to show his amusement as his secretary walked in and placed the blank search-warrant on the desk before returning to her own office.

'I have known Mayor Ben Kildare for ten years, gentlemen,' said the judge. 'This is not his handwriting and certainly not his signature.'

Wild Bill rested his knuckles on the desk and stared down at the bemused judge.

'Are you sure, sir?'

'Yes, Marshal. I am positive. Whoever wrote this letter, it was not the mayor.'

Hickok turned his head to look at Dix and Shaw. 'Someone is playing games, Dixie.'

'Where is this place, Judge?' asked Dix. 'I've never heard of Painted Rock.'

'Painted Rock is roughly ten miles east of Cheyenne,' D.L. Cooper answered. 'A remote canyon trail. An ideal place for ruthless men to get the better of innocent riders who try to get through its barren heart.'

Hickok rose up to his full height.

'An ambush!'

'Reckon so,' said Dix. He turned to say something to Rufas Harper but the sheriff had gone. 'I see Rufas has gone. I wonder why?'

Hickok ran his fingers down his moustache.

'I think that we ought to go take us a ride to this Painted Rock, Dixie.'

Tom Dix nodded in agreement. 'Yep.'

Judge Cooper stood and pulled his pipe from his lips.

'Are you sure that's wise, Marshal?'

'Maybe not, sir. But someone has got to bite the bullet and take a few risks if we're ever going to catch the brand-burners and their leader.'

The judge dipped his pen into a large inkwell and signed the search warrant. He turned it over and rubbed it on his blotter. He handed it to the marshal.

'Surely it would be a far safer course to take if you just checked out the ownership of the brand that you are seeking, Marshal Hickok?'

'I guess so, sir,' Wild Bill agreed. 'The trouble is, I've a feeling that if I can get my hands on those rustlers, they might spill the beans and point us in the right direction. Frightened men can be mighty talkative.'

Judge Cooper nodded in agreement. He had heard a lot about Hickok and knew it was pointless trying to argue with the tall marshal.

'Who am I to disagree with the famed Wild Bill Hickok?' The judge sat down, placed his pipe in an ashtray and folded his arms. 'I'm sure you know what you are doing. I hope so, anyway.'

Hickok touched the brim of his Stetson, and then handed the warrant to Dan Shaw.

'You check out them brands, Dan. Me and Dixie will take us a ride to see who it is wants us to believe that he's the mayor of this town.'

Dan Shaw tried to protest. 'But I ought to ride with you boys, Bill.'

Tom Dix patted Dan's broad back and gave him his crude drawing of the brand that had been burned on to the hides of three of their steers.

'Whoever sent this note is expecting just two riders, Dan. I reckon three would scare the critters off. You go and try to find out who owns this brand.'

'When I do, I'll come after you at top speed,' Dan vowed.

Dix smiled and turned to face Hickok.

'Ready, Dixie?' Hickok asked.

'Yep, James Butler,' Dix said. 'I'm ready.'

FOURTEEN

The two horsemen used their reins to whip the shoulders of their trusty mounts as they galloped ever closer to Painted Rock. They had travelled nearly ten miles when they saw the strange rock formation ahead of their horses, catching the last rays of the setting sun.

They could see why this place had earned its name. A myriad of colours danced over the high granite monolith as the fading sunlight gradually sank.

Both riders felt uneasy as they drew closer and closer to the place where they were meant to meet Mayor Ben Kildare. They knew that if ever something had been created that was a perfect spot to ambush unsuspecting riders, Painted Rock was it.

Hickok was the first to drag back on his reins

and stop his tall stallion. Dix had been trailing the US marshal, now he brought his quarter horse to a standstill beside his friend.

Hickok stood in his stirrups and stared ahead at the black trees that stood before the large rugged rock, and at the canyon trail beyond.

Dix turned his mount full circle and faced the lawman.

'What ya thinking, Bill?'

'I'm thinking that it'll be dark before we reach the canyon, Dixie,' replied Hickok.

'Is that good or bad?' asked Dixie.

James Butler had no answer to that question. He lowered himself on to the beautiful saddle and pulled out a long thin cigar from his jacket pocket. Dix watched the man bite off the end of the cigar and spit it at the ground.

'The darkness might help us get the drop on them, Bill.'

Hickok nodded. He struck a match on his saddle horn and cupped the flame in his hands. He puffed thoughtfully and then inhaled deeply.

'How many of them brand-burners are there, Dixie?'

'I seen about eight as I recall,' replied Dix, his mind drifting back to the previous night. 'Only one of them seemed to know how to handle his guns, though.'

Hickok nodded again.

'Reckon the rest of them are just cowboys.

Cowboys who've dipped their hands in the cookie-jar.'

'That's what I was thinking,' Dix agreed.

Hickok blew a line of smoke at the ground.

'But even cowboys can bushwhack folks.'

Dix dismounted, removed his full canteen from the saddle horn and unscrewed the stopper.

'I'll water the horses.'

Hickok remained silent, his keen senses surveying the area ahead of them. He rose in his saddle, then eased himself off the back of the tall chestnut.

'I've got me an idea, Dixie.'

Tom Dix dropped his hat on the ground and poured some water into its large bowl. He glanced through the half-light at his brooding companion.

'Is it a good idea, Bill?'

'Damn good!'

The seven chimes of the big clock high above the town hall rang out. Dan Shaw had used the search warrant to enter the locked office of the Cattlemen's Association inside the town hall more than an hour earlier. He had not realized that there would be so many registered brands lying in the bank of filing cabinets.

For not only was every one of the Wyoming brands carefully marked on the small index cards, but those from almost all the other territories and states filled box after box.

Daylight had helped him for the first three boxes but now it was dark inside the small wood-panelled room. Dan struck a match and touched the wick of a large oil-lamp on the desk. Then he placed the glass bowl and funnel back into position. The small room filled with light as the rancher carefully opened another box.

He thought about Dix and Wild Bill. This was taking him far longer than he had imagined it would.

Yet if the brand he was looking for was here, he was determined to find it. Even if it took all night.

Dan watched as smoke rose from the badly adjusted wick of the lamp and knew that he would have to open the window before it filled the small room. He reached up and flicked a metal catch across and pushed the solitary window open. Cold air rushed in and cooled him down.

He glanced into the alley which ran along the side of the red-brick building. It was dark and had an aroma he did not relish.

Dan returned to the desk and began to check the next box of cards. His eyes were tired after having examined more than 200 of the three-by-four-inch cards.

Then a noise outside the window drew his attention. He turned and looked up. At first he did not see what had alerted him. He pushed his hat-brim up until it rested on the crown of his head.

Then he saw it.

A gun barrel aimed straight at him through the open window.

The lamplight glistened across the barrel of the cocked weapon. Dan Shaw ducked and drew both his guns, but it was too late. A gunshot blasted through the window. The small room filled with deafening noise as the bullet shattered the oil-filled glass bowl of the lamp.

A blinding flash of light erupted on the desk as liquid flames ran like water in every direction. Flames rose to the ceiling as the varnished wooden filing-cabinets were soaked in the blazing kerosene.

Dan fired at the window with both his guns. The glass smashed and went cascading into the dark alley. But whoever had fired into the small room was long gone.

Flames erupted all around him.

Blistering heat forced him to move backward as choking smoke billowed from the disintegrating cabinets, table and chair. The rancher holstered his guns and pulled his gloves from his coat pockets and put them on. He loosened his bandanna and covered his mouth and nose.

The entire room seemed to groan in agony as its panelling felt the unchecked fury of the inferno.

The ceiling was alight above his head and molten varnish was raining down on the crouching figure.

Dan Shaw's mind raced as he tried to make sense of the situation in which he suddenly found himself.

Who had fired that gun?

Had they been aiming at him?

Perhaps the oil-lamp had been their target.

Was the single bullet meant to kill him or just to burn all evidence of the cattle brands?

Shaw pulled his coat-collar up and his hat brim down. He tried to make his way out of the room and into the great marble hall of the building. Then he heard a cracking sound above him. He paused and looked up.

The ceiling had turned into a blanket of fire.

The heavy boards which had covered the room were now nothing more than charcoal. Dan raised his hands and tried to shield his face from the heat and flames that came from everywhere. The sound stopped him once again.

It sounded as if a tree was falling.

In a way, that was exactly what it was.

Blackened joists moved as the weighty heavy furniture in the room directly above the Cattlemen's Association office began to break through.

It was raining fire.

Dan looked all around him as smoke filled his lungs. He went to run towards the open doorway when a massive blazing desk fell out of the smoke and crashed in front of him. The door was now alight too.

The rancher backed away and turned again.

There was desperation in his every heartbeat. He tried to see through the blinding smoke, to find another way out. Was there another door? His gloved hands tore at the furniture all around him and threw it at the ground. He patted the walls as it became harder and harder to see anything.

He could smell varnish burning on the cabinets. He coughed as his lungs vainly tried to expel the deadly fumes.

Dan raised his left hand to cover his face and groped along the wall with his right. A chilling realization dawned on him.

There was only one way in and out of this room.

The door, which was blocked by blazing furniture and joists, was the only door in this room. He felt dizzy as the acrid smoke continued to fill his lungs. The rancher staggered and fell to his knees.

The heat was incredible. Dan felt as if he were being roasted on a spit.

He fell flat on his face and lay motionless for a

few seconds. As he began to lose his battle with consciousness he felt the flames licking out at him across the floor.

Dan rolled away and used his gloves to extinguish the fire that had ignited on his coat. Then saw the window above him.

Smoke was curling out through the broken panes as fresh air tried to fight its way in past the flames.

Dan Shaw narrowed his eyes and stared at it for what felt like an eternity. He tried to breathe but there was no air that had not been filled with the black deadly smoke.

He knew that if he did not get out through that hole in the wall within the next few moments, he would die.

Dan forced himself up off the floor of the room, hauled his coat off his back and held it in front of his face. He ran with all his strength and leapt.

The sound of the remaining window panes breaking as he threw himself at them filled his ears. Then he felt the pain of the sharp glass splinters ripping into his flesh.

He had no time to yell out in agony.

Dan Shaw hit the ground hard. He tried to get up but there was no strength left in his weakened body. A bottomless pool of darkness overwhelmed him. He fell into it helplessly.

*

Mac Mason made his way down through the rocks that overlooked the narrow canyon. He had placed his eight fellow-brand-burners around the middle of the mile long pass. Some were up high in the crags like himself, whilst others were nearer the ground secreted behind large boulders.

The trap had been set.

A large blazing torch had been driven into the ground in the centre of the canyon. This was meant to slow the two riders long enough for Mason and his men to strike.

It was a simple plan.

When Dix and his partner rode along the canyon to meet Ben Kildare, they would see the torch. When they stopped, Mason's men would rope the pair and haul them off their saddles.

Then the brand-burners would keep shooting until the two ranchers were dead.

The element of surprise and volume of lead would ensure that they satisfied the orders of their boss.

The rustlers had been waiting since just before sunset, after Pete Walker had returned from delivering the note to Sheriff Harper's office.

The brand-burners were nervous. Every passing second made them even more aware of who it was that they were waiting for. Tom Dix was a deadly gunfighter. Even the white hair and wrinkled face could not alter that fact. When he fired his guns, he usually hit what he was aiming at.

Mason clambered down the rocks until he reached the floor of the canyon. He rested a hand on Eli Payne's shoulder.

'Get ready with that rope, Eli,' growled Mason into the man's ear. 'I want you to put that old lasso over their heads. You then haul the critters off their horses. Once you get a rope on them, the other boys will do the rest. Understand?'

Payne did not reply.

His mouth was too dry to form any words that could fall from his cracked lips. The canyon was filled with black shadows and only the flames that licked off the torch, a hundred feet away from them, gave any light within the confines of the rocky corridor. Payne looked up at the massive rock which jutted into the star-filled sky.

He wondered whether it might be their tombstone.

Mason screwed up his eyes. Every one of the brand-burners was in his hiding place. Larry Brady was high above them, opposite, with a Winchester. Travis, Smith and Walker were huddled on the ground with their own lariats in readiness to follow up after Eli Payne had roped the two riders.

Toby Dwayne and Jeb Olsen were ten feet above Mason with guns in their nervous hands. Sam Canute held on to a double-barrelled scattergun as he knelt behind the torch.

Mac Mason was about to move when he heard the sound of horses' hoofs echoing off the granite rocks. He lowered himself down behind Payne.

'They're coming, boys.'

All eight men squinted into the darkness and waited. Every man was scared. Scared of the unseen prey. A prey whom he knew was capable of destroying every one of them.

FIFTEEN

James Butler Hickok reached the top of the canyon wall and stared down into the shadows. He could see the blazing torch stuck into the ground far below him and the kneeling figure behind it. His hooded eyes surveyed the scene carefully as he descended into the canyon. One by one he noted the position of the brand-burners as his long legs negotiated the rugged rock-face.

Then he saw the dust rising out of the blackness of the trail and smiled to himself.

Dix had done exactly as instructed.

The veteran gunfighter had allowed Hickok exactly twenty minutes to climb the high wall of rock before he started along the dark canyon. Dix had both their mounts tied together and was riding his smaller quarter horse in readiness for when he encountered the gang of rustlers.

Every sinew in the rider's body was tense.

Tom Dix prayed that he and Hickok were wrong, that there was no trap awaiting him in the heart of the canyon. He did not want to have to use his prized Colt Peacemakers again.

For time had matured the once deadly gunfighter.

He no longer took pleasure in ending the lives of less capable gunmen, no matter how evil they were.

Wild Bill Hickok had moved down the wall of rock, unseen by the men who lay in wait with an arsenal of weaponry and cutting-ropes in their sweating hands. He was now standing half-way between the canyon floor and the top of the rocky ridge. He could see that Dix had almost reached the bushwhackers.

There was no time to lose.

Hickok had to act now.

He pulled both his pistols from their holsters and eased their hammers back until they locked.

Larry Brady was closest, then came Dave Travis, Cal Smith and Pete Walker huddled close together. Each had his gun and rifle in his hands.

Hickok kicked at the gravel at his feet. He watched silently as it showered over the four rustlers.

Four startled men turned and looked up in horror at the tall elegant figure above them. The brand-burners cocked and aimed their guns.

Hickok opened up.

The lethal accuracy of his weapons did not fail the US marshal. All four men were dead within a few seconds.

Hearing the shots, Tom Dix jumped from his saddle and allowed the two horses to continue. He drew his matched pair of Colts and ran through the shadows after them. The dust that spewed up from their hoofs gave him all the cover he needed.

Mac Mason watched in horror as four of his men fell from the rock-face into the canyon. Instinctively, he cocked his own guns and fired.

But Hickok was gone.

'What's happening?' Payne asked.

'Just rope them riders, Eli,' ordered Mason as his eyes searched vainly for the man who had killed half his gang in less than a heartbeat.

The sound of the approaching horses grew louder. Eli Payne stood and swung the rope over his head in total obedience. As the two horses galloped out of the blackness towards him he released his grip and watched as the loop of rope flew over the necks of the two horses. Payne's expert hands wrapped the long tail of the rope around his shoulder, then pulled back hard.

As the loop tightened around the necks of the galloping horses, he realized that neither had riders on their saddles.

'Where are they, Mac?' a confused Payne called out. 'These nags are empty.'

'What's goin' on?' Mason screamed in a mixture of anger and fear.

Olsen and Dwayne came rushing down from their hiding-places to where Mason and Payne were standing. A cloud of dust swept over them as Payne's rope stopped the horses.

'Who killed Pete and the boys, Mac?' asked a terrified Jeb Olsen.

Dwayne pointed at the shadowy rock opposite them.

'I see someone up there, but then he just vanished.'

There was no time for Mason to reply.

Suddenly out of the dust came Tom Dix with his cocked guns in his gloved hands. The gunfighter stopped and faced the four men who stood less than twenty feet ahead of him.

Dix noted that Eli Payne was holding on to his rope and making no effort to go for his holstered gun. The three other men were a different matter, though. They had their primed weapons aimed straight at him.

'We meet again, old-timer,' Mason called out.

Dix gritted his teeth.

'Reckon so, sonny.'

A deafening shot rang out from behind the brand-burners. They all turned and looked at Sam Canute as he staggered away from the burning torch, clutching his middle before falling face down in the dust.

Wild Bill Hickok walked out of the shadows towards the group of brand-burners.

'Don't you just hate it when an old-fashioned bushwhackin' goes wrong, boys?' the marshal asked.

'What the hell is that?' Olsen gasped.

Toby Dwayne was shaking.

'If'n I didn't know better, I'd say that was Wild Bill Hickok, boys.'

Mac Mason felt sweat running down his spine.

'Hickok? It can't be.'

Tom Dix whistled and drew their attention.

'Ya wrong, sonny. That is the famed Wild Bill.'

Mac Mason's eyes darted back and forth between the two gunfighting legends. He swallowed hard. They were both closing in on him and what was left of his men.

'Drop them hoglegs and you'll live,' Hickok said firmly.

'We gotta fight, boys!' Mason growled. 'There ain't no other way. If we don't fight, they'll hang us anyway in Cheyenne. I'd rather die shootin' than have my neck stretched.'

Dwayne and Olsen moved nervously to Mason's the side.

'Then we fight!' Olsen spat.

Eli Payne released his grip on the cutting rope and dropped to the ground.

'I ain't fighting, Mac. I'd rather hang than go up against these critters. Tom Dix is bad enough but what chance is there against Wild Bill Hickok?'

Mac Mason turned and looked down on the man sobbing at his feet.

'You're just a yella jinx, Eli.'

Both Dix and Hickok watched in disbelief when Mason fired at the kneeling man. Payne slumped over limply.

'Just as I reckoned. You're vermin!' Hickok shouted angrily across the distance between them.

'Only scum kills their own, James Butler,' Dix agreed.

'Kill 'em!' Mason shouted at the top of his voice. 'Kill 'em before they start preaching from the Good Book.'

The canyon was lit up by the flashes from the barrels of the guns in all the men's hands. The ear-splitting noise bounced off all the ragged granite walls as the acrid aroma of gunsmoke filled the night air.

It was a fight which ended a mere handful of seconds after it had started. The silence which trailed in its wake was familiar to the two gunfighters.

Wild Bill Hickok and Tom Dix were the only

men standing amid the carnage when the gunsmoke cleared. They approached the bodies as they holstered their guns.

'I hate this, Bill,' Dix admitted.

'You and me both, Dixie.' Hickok sighed. 'Sometimes there just ain't no other way, though.'

'It still tastes bad.'

Before Hickok could agree he suddenly noticed Eli Payne's left hand moving amid the other bodies. He knelt and turned the man's head until their eyes met.

'Are you the real Wild Bill?' Payne's faint voice asked.

Hickok nodded.

'Yep, partner. I'm Wild Bill.'

'I wanted no part of this.' Payne gasped as he felt his life slipping away from him. 'It was the boss back in Cheyenne. He reckoned Tom Dix was close to finding out his name. He ordered us to kill him and his pal. Mac threatened to kill us if we didn't ambush Dix.'

Hickok nodded.

'I could tell that you ain't never fired that gun in anger, friend.'

Tom Dix knelt down next to Hickok who cradled the head of the dying man in his arms.

'What's the name of your boss?'

Eli Payne gestured to Hickok with his fingers. Wild Bill leaned down until his ear was close to the rustler's lips.

Dix noticed as Payne's hand dropped limply to the ground. As Hickok's noble head rose, he looked straight at him.

'Did he tell you who the boss of the brand-burners is, James Butler?

'Yep.'

FINALE

The two riders had seen the glowing embers rising up into the star-filled sky on their long ride back to Cheyenne from Painted Rock. It had guided them like a beacon back to the cattle town. Countless eyes watched as Hickok and Dix steered their tired mounts through the winding streets. They knew where they were going and who it was that the dying Eli Payne had named as the boss of the brand-burners.

Smoke traced its way past the horsemen as they noticed a familiar figure ahead of them. Train whistles from the railhead cut through the night air as the riders reined in and watched the approaching Seth Green waving feverishly.

'Where have ya been? Me and Rufas have looked everywhere for ya both,' gasped Green.

Dix and Hickok ignored the question.

'What's on fire?' Dix asked as he stood in his stirrups and stared down the long wide street.

The deputy sheriff rested a hand on the bridle of the tall chestnut stallion.

'The town hall. We managed to put it out but half the building is gone,' replied Green.

Dix moved his horse closer to the deputy.

'Anyone hurt?'

'That's why I stopped ya both. Ya pal got himself caught in there and is over at Doc Parker's.'

Hickok leaned down.

'Is he hurt bad?'

'Nope. He was cut jumping out of a window and sucked in a lot of smoke but the doc managed to fix him up,' answered Green. 'He gave him a sleeping draught. The doc reckons he'll be OK tomorrow.'

Dix looked at Hickok and nodded. The US marshal returned the gesture. Both men spurred their mounts and rode off into the smoke-filled street.

'Where you boys goin'?' Green called out.

There was no reply.

The Little Dice saloon was even busier than usual as scores of men tried to wash the taste of smoke from their mouths after helping to put out the fire in the town hall. None of them noticed the two grim-faced horsemen who drew up directly outside the swing-doors.

Hickok dismounted and stepped up on to the boardwalk as Tom Dix threw his right leg over his horse's head and slid to the ground. Hickok made good use of the time as he waited for the exhausted Dix to catch up with him. He removed all the spent shells from his guns and then reloaded.

'Somebody in here is bound to know where he is, Dixie.'

'You sure about this, Bill?' asked Dix. He checked his own guns. 'We only got the word of a dying cowboy that he's the boss of the brand-burners.'

'Yep. I'm sure, Dixie. I never met a dying man who didn't tell the truth,' replied Hickok. He holstered his guns and pushed his way into the saloon. 'C'mon.'

The two men walked across the sawdust-covered floor until they reached the busy bar. Hickok hauled men out of his way and then snapped his fingers at the bartender.

'Bottle of whiskey!' he demanded.

The bartender saw Dix standing next to Hickok and pulled a bottle of his best-labelled whiskey from the shelf behind him. He placed two thimble glasses down and forced a fearful smile.

'On the house, gents.'

'Much obliged,' said Hickok. He pulled the cork from the neck of the bottle with his teeth and spat it at the floor. He poured two glasses. 'Drink up, Dixie.'

Tom Dix watched as his friend downed his drink in one swift movement and then poured another.

He pulled out a scrap of paper and a two-inch pencil and scribbled a name on to it. He showed it to the bartender.

'Do you know where he is?'

The bartender read the name and nodded.

'Upstairs, Mr Dix. He's upstairs as is his nightly habit.'

Dix sipped at his whiskey, then patted Hickok's shoulder.

'He's upstairs, Bill.'

Hickok finished another drink, then placed his glass over the neck of the bottle.

'Which room?'

The bartender gulped and held four fingers up.

'Four?' Hickok checked.

'Yes, sir. Four.'

Hickok and Dix pushed their way through the crowd and up the carpeted staircase until they reached the well-illuminated landing. They paused and studied the doors. The room with the number four painted on its surface was right in front of them. They strode towards it at speed.

Dix drew one of his guns, then kicked at the door with all his strength. The lock remained, but the door splintered off its hinges and landed on the end of the occupied bed before it slid off the brass tail-board on to the floor.

The two men hurriedly followed the busted door into the room and saw a half-naked female. She threw herself from the bed, and then crawled out between them. She did not stop crawling until she reached the sanctuary of another room.

Tom Dix aimed his pistol at the lump beneath the large bedspread as Hickok rested his hands on his crossed gungrips and stared hard at the hidden figure.

'If you don't get out of that bed, Deputy Dix here will surely kill you,' said the marshal, quietly.

Slowly the sheets were lowered.

Hickok stepped closer to the brass bedposts. He inhaled and shook his head as if in disappointment.

'Who'd have figured it was you?'

Judge D.L. Cooper glared at the two men.

'What do you mean, Mr Hickok? What are you accusing me of, exactly?'

'You're the varmint behind the brand-burners, Judge. It's you who's been making your fortune out of the honest ranchers in and around Cheyenne. You're the boss.'

D.L. Cooper smiled.

'Am I?'

Dix lowered his gun. 'The game's up, Judge. One of your brand-burners told us everything.'

Cooper glanced at Dix briefly.

'And where is this talkative man, Mr Dix?'

'Dead! Like the rest of them,' snapped Hickok as he walked around the room.

The judge smiled even more.

'Then you have no proof at all.'

Dix rested a boot on the end of the soft mattress and looked at the elderly man in total disbelief.

'He told Wild Bill and Wild Bill will testify to that in a court of law, sir.'

Hickok moved to the window and pulled the drapes away. His hooded eyes stared out at the still-glowing town hall and the few remaining men who were throwing buckets of water at it.

'You managed to burn the brand registrations, I take it? You almost killed our pal Dan Shaw as well.'

'I did?' Judge Cooper tried to look innocent. He was good at that. For some reason the elderly judge had found that most people trusted old people with snow-white hair.

Hickok continued to stare through the window-panes, his back to the judge.

'Yep. You sure did. And when the folks at Dodge City get my wire they'll send me a copy of your registered brand on the next train.'

Dix walked to the side of the marshal. 'They will?'

'Sure, Dixie.' Wild Bill sighed. 'You see, they got copies in all the major cattle towns. All we have to do is arrest this critter and wait for the Dodge train.'

Suddenly the sheets moved. Hickok watched the reflection in the windowpane as the judge hauled out his pistol and aimed it the backs of the two lawmen.

He squeezed its trigger. The bullet passed between the two men and went straight through the top pane of glass.

Faster than the blink of an eye, Wild Bill turned, drew one of his guns and fanned its hammer twice.

The elderly judge was hit in the chest by both bullets and slumped sideways. The sheets turned red as blood soaked into them.

Hickok blew the barrel of his gun and slid it back into its holster. He then led Dix back out on to the landing. They looked down into the saloon. It was silent as every face stared up at them. The door to room 'one' opened and a half-dressed Sheriff Harper staggered out with a gun in his hand.

'You again?' Harper asked as his eyes caught sight of the body in the bed inside room four. 'Who you killed now?'

Hickok smiled. He looked at the sheriff.

'I killed Judge Cooper, Rufas. Any objections?'

'I give up. I'm gonna quit this damn job.' Harper lowered his weapon and shook his head.

The two men started to walk down the carpeted staircase as the sheriff returned to his room. The door slammed.

'Let's go see Dan.'

'But Seth said he was asleep.' Dix holstered his gun.

'Then he ought to be a darn sight quieter than he usually is, Dixie.' Hickok grinned.

Tom Dix watched as the patrons parted like the Red Sea before them. Hickok grabbed the bottle from the bar counter and continued out into the cool evening air.

'When did you send that wire to Dodge, Bill?' Dix asked as they stepped down into the street and picked their reins up off the ground.

'What wire, Dixie?' Hickok raised an eyebrow.

'You've still got vinegar, James Butler.' Dix laughed.

'Yep. I reckon you're right, Dixie.'